# The Migrant and
# The Maverick

*An Allegory*

Other books by
ABIE ALEXANDER

AN AMERICAN IN SEARCH OF GOD
CHASING THE WIND
SOMETIMES WHEN WE MEET
MEMORIES AND MIRAGES
FOR THE LOVE OF ARMINE
OF MINGLED YARN

# The Migrant and The Maverick

## An Allegory

# Abie Alexander

AA
BOOKS

Copyright © 2016 Abie Alexander

*First Published 2017*

| | |
|---|---|
| *Print* | 978-1-946593-28-3 |
| *EPUB* | 978-1-946593-29-0 |
| *AZW3* | 978-1-946593-30-6 |
| *MOBI* | 978-1-946593-31-3 |
| *PDF* | 978-1-946593-32-0 |

Published in the United States of America

AA
BOOKS

7919 Mandan Road #103
Greenbelt, Maryland. USA 20770-2828
+1 (301) 335-5632
*aa-books@outlook.com*
*www.abiealexander.com*

This book is dedicated to:


all immigrants who reinvent their lives in
multifarious ways in foreign lands, braving
storms,
torrents, sharp stones, shards of glass, fiery
coals,
and even serpents, en route to attaining
their destinies against insurmountable odds;


and, to:


Mr. Karen Babahanov, the Aren of the book,
in admiration and with respect.

"Why should a man be scorned if, finding himself in prison, he tries to get out and go home? Or if, when he cannot do so, he thinks and talks about other topics than jailers and prison-walls?"

J.R.R. Tolkien, On Fairy-Stories

"Someday you will be old enough to start reading fairy tales again."

C.S. Lewis, Letter to his goddaughter, Lucy

# TABLE OF CONTENTS

# 1 THE FOREIGNERS HAVE ARRIVED!

His mother was right. She was always right.

There they were—the immigrants—by the edge of the green pond.

A few were stretching themselves languorously in the morning sun. The others seemed to be having fun swimming around in the cold pond, splashing water on each other or dunking their heads below the surface. Even from this distance, they appeared to be larger and stronger than his kindred, yet graceful and beautiful. Most importantly, they looked so different!

'How in the world can they love these icy cold waters?' wondered Ken.

Then he saw her.

It was love at first sight.

There she stood, a short distance away from the others, daintily on one foot, the other coyly tucked under her, oblivious of everything around her—her team-mates, the pond, and the grove of trees by the water's edge.

Ken hurried back indoors to tell his mother what he had just seen.

"You were right, Ma," Ken said excitedly. "The foreigners are here! They are big and different. They are enormous! They are giants! And they are bathing in the pond. They don't seem to mind the cold at all."

"It is much colder where they've come from. That's the reason they come here to winter. Our cold is nothing to them. The winters up north are bleak and harsh. Everything is frozen for many weeks, even months, in some places far north. Totally inhospitable."

She smiled as she added, "I expect they consider this warm."

Ken recalled how Ma had abruptly risen from their midst the previous night and walked over to the wooden wall of their shack to listen intently.

Ken had not heard a thing. He and his siblings were fast sleepers, huddling close to their mother through the night, oblivious of the goings-on in the world outside. But unlike the others, Ken would awaken the instant Ma shifted around.

"How did you know, Ma, without actually seeing them, that they arrived?" asked Ken now.

"You don't have to see everything with your eyes. Some things come to you unsought. You just know," she explained mysteriously.

After a pause, she added, "I knew they would come. This land—this world—is as much theirs as it is ours. You had better hurry out and finish your breakfast. I'll be out in a few minutes."

Ma laid an egg every single day unlike his lazy aunts who skipped an egg every so often. But not Ma.

When Ken stepped out of the shack there was no one to be seen. The whole group had dispersed over the meadow rummaging for more food. They always scrambled and jostled each other for the corn that Ryan, the youngest child of the house, scattered before them every morning. The grain would disappear in a flurry of furious pecking and fierce competition. Ryan loved to watch them swarm around his legs gobbling greedily. He would fling the corn in arcs to his left and then to his right or straight ahead, and the whole brood would scurry over there even if there was still grain left over at the previous spot.

All except Ken. Ryan loved Ken the most. Ken was his pet. And Ken loved Ryan in return. Actually, the whole flock loved Ryan. Of all in the McGuire family, Ryan was the clear favorite of Ken and his group. While the rest of the family slept, Ryan was the first out of the house every morning, with a mug of corn in his hand to feed the brood. They all loved him, but none more than Ken.

Ryan had noticed early on that Ken was not getting his fair share of the corn. The other males, jealous of Ken's special status with Ryan, would gang up to attack Ken and drive him away. Ken protected himself agilely when the assailants got too close, but he did not strike back. He was a dreamer and a pacifist, and he considered fighting over food the worst battle for a peaceable person.

Ryan had devised a plan that Ken quickly cottoned on to. Once the others were frantically engaged in pecking, Ryan would signal Ken and saunter around the corner, past the tire trough of water, to quietly serve Ken's extra portion behind the tall water drum, out of sight of the others. This way Ken got the quantity of food he needed without having to fight for it.

On that fateful day, Ken was in the middle of his private breakfast when he had heard the unfamiliar cackle of the immigrants. Recalling Ma getting up in the middle of the night, he had left his morning meal midway to take a look at the newcomers from the edge of the chain-link fence before racing back to share the news with Ma. Now as he stepped out again, his breakfast was still there, just as he had left it.

Ken polished off the remnants in a trice. He did not want to join the others to forage for food this morning. His mind was on the foreigners by the pond who had braved the journey of a thousand miles, as Ma had told them they would, a few days earlier. He felt happy. Today was a special day. The foreigners had arrived. Gorging could wait.

So, he drew himself up to his full height, and arching his neck, sang a full-throated, 'Oh, What A Beautiful Morning!'

Ken was a splendid singer. His voice had broken into a deep baritone a few weeks earlier. Whenever Ryan heard Ken's spirited singing, even when indoors preparing for school, he would smile broadly. Ken's song today was so full of optimism that it made Ryan look eagerly forward to the promise of a new day.

His morning anthem done, Ken walked over to the fence again. He cocked his head to get a better look through the chain-link fence.

There she was again. 'Boy, is she beautiful!'

Ken was smitten by the pitch-black head, the snow-white chinstrap, long black neck, the dark-brown wings, and the fawn colored breast and midriff.

In a way that he could not explain, she stood apart, a cut above the rest, distinctly more poised than the others, almost royal in her demeanor.

There was something sensuous about her stance as well. She seemed to favor standing on one leg like a sinuous ballerina, perfectly straight, with nary a tilt.

For the first time in his life, Ken felt the stirrings of love. The fact that they belonged to different tribes, and hence any real love improbable, or even impossible, did not cross his mind.

He gazed spellbound as she preened herself, daintily pecking at her half-stretched wings. She seemed to sense that she was being watched and stopped abruptly midway to look around. Ken wanted to run away and hide.

It was too late. She had seen him.

For a long minute, they both stared at each other.

Then, as he watched transfixed, she straightened up, flapped her arms, and was serenely airborne in his direction. She made an elegant two-point landing about six feet from the fence, her outstretched deep-brown wings, a gesture of openness, the defenseless cream and tan midriff, a symbol of trust. She walked the last few steps to come closer to the barrier.

"Hello, I am Helen," she said in a mellifluous voice that was music to Ken's ears.

Ken found his voice with some difficulty. "Hi! I'm Ke ... Ke ... Ken," he stuttered.

"Nice day, eh?" said Helen conversationally.

"Yeah, it sure is. Are you a foreigner?" blurted out Ken. He cringed when he realized the implications of what he had just said.

Helen only smiled amusedly.

Her smile was a smile that could light up an entire field like moonlight on a cloudless night or sunflowers on a sunny day.

"I didn't mean to be rude," Ken hastened to add. "Ma told us you all came from another country, a thousand miles away."

"And she's right. I'm a Canada goose from St. Catharines." Seeing the blank look on Ken's face, she added, "Ontario, Canada."

"Ah! And I'm a Rhode Island Red from ..." Ken paused, shrugging his pinions in a self-deprecating shrug, "I'm from around here. Greenbelt, actually. Prince Georges county, Maryland."

"Don't be embarrassed about being a local. It's no great shakes being an expat."

"An expat? How is that different from a refugee?"

"So that's what they call us, eh?" chuckled Helen.

"I didn't mean it that way ..." began Ken, mortified again at his own gaffe. He slapped his forehead with his right wing.

"No offense taken!" Helen pondered for a moment before continuing. "Come to think of it, there's not much of a difference, really. Expats are just refugees in disguise."

It took a minute for that to register. When it did, Ken burst out laughing. "Why do you say that?"

"Most expats—not all, mind—are either attention-seeking domestic discards who cannot find a decent job in their home country or wolves in sheep's clothing who prey on the poverty, conflicts, and travails of the less fortunate in poorer countries. They are mostly social misfits who think their amateur sociology can save the South, and maybe even the North. They go where the money is. They are mercy-pretenders. Old imperialism in new clothing, that's what it is. If it was in fact pity that moved them, there's enough misery in their own backyard, right under their very noses. Why go all the way to Sub-Saharan Africa or Haiti?"

"That's not at all what Ma told us about your ilk. She had only the nicest words for you. She told us all how polite, industrious, and adventurous your tribe is. But for some reason, human beings have a love-hate relationship with you. She said you are unfairly maligned. That you are more sinned against than sinning."

"Your mother is kind. Actually, I consider myself neither an expat nor a refugee. I am what I am—wherever I may be. We are neither aliens here nor foreigners there. This entire world belongs to all of us," Helen said, spreading her wings out expansively.

"That's exactly what Ma said!" exclaimed Ken. "This world is everyone's!"

"Your mother is an enlightened lady. You are fortunate to be her son."

"That I sure am! I love her to bits. She knows so much. She teaches us something new every day.

She told us that we could communicate with any other living being. And she was right. Here I am talking to you just arrived from a thousand miles away! And what's more, we can understand each other!"

"I don't find that surprising at all. We both may speak a little differently. But we can get through to each other a hundred per cent, eh?"

"I have no problem comprehending you, Helen. I did not even notice you spoke differently."

Helen smiled. "It is xenophobia that accentuates the disparities and uses languages as walls, pushing them farther apart. In the beginning, there was just one universal language that everyone spoke."

"But I can't understand a word those crows or blue jays say! They seem to be talking code!"

"You will—if you keep your mind open. If I were to take a wild guess, I'd say that you do not find them attractive or desirable company?" Helen probed gently.

"Yes, that I confess. The crows are uncouth, ill-mannered, destructive, and disorderly. And the blue jays are noisy and garrulous," Ken did not hide his distaste.

"See, that's where the problem lies. Not in the

language. I'm a polyglot myself. The more languages you know, the more open you become to other cultures."

"Where did you learn my language?" asked Ken.

"Oh, I learned chicken-speak in St. Catharines. But you don't have to cross continents to learn other tongues. Though, I must admit the first time I heard the clucking of a mother hen, it sounded like the click language of the San Bushmen!"

"Very droll. Are you all from Canada?" Ken was curious.

"Our team here is from Canada. But you could find Canada geese in other countries as well."

"I thought you were all Canadians!" exclaimed Ken.

Helen smiled broadly. "Sometimes people mistakenly call us Canadian geese instead of Canada geese. We are not all Canadian. Some of us are American. And, as I said, there are other nationalities as well."

"Really?"

"Yes. On the diaspora ratings, only the Armenians come anywhere close to us. You can find us in England and in parts of Europe as well. Even in Russia, as far away as the Kamchatka

Peninsula in the Far East."

Just then there was a shout from the pond's edge.

"Sorry, got to run. Clean forgot about the debrief meeting. We do that after every long trip."

Ken was loath to see her go. Reluctantly he said, "Nice to have met you. I hope to see you again soon."

"Likewise. But remember, we birds are all one—irrespective of plumage, language, lineage, heritage, or any other kind of age!" Helen smiled before continuing. "Subdivisions amongst us are an abomination."

"That's deep," Ken said shaking his head.

"So long, my newfound friend!" With that Helen levitated herself over the fence and gently floated in a downward loop to the water's edge where her group had assembled.

Ken dreamed of faraway lands that night.

## 2  Hobnobbing With The Immigrant

The next morning, Ken had more than his usual fill at breakfast. He was dying to meet Helen again and spend as much time as possible in her company. He did not want to have to leave her side to come back for a bite to eat or a gulp of water to drink. So, he decided to stuff himself before leaving home. He would happily spend the entire day with her, if she allowed, he told himself.

With this plan, Ken hung around Ryan for a second helping. Ryan picked him up and, cradling him in the crook of his left arm, gently stroked Ken's shiny red and black plumes with his right hand. After a while, Ryan held Ken up with both hands and placed him gently on his right shoulder.

From this high perch, he was a sight to behold! The mahogany-black feathers shimmered in the morning sun. The yellow toes dug into the red-and black scotch plaid shirt that Ryan had on.

Ryan lightly touched Ken's comb with his right hand. That was Ken's cue. He shook his dark red and black mane and flapped his arms once, as if calling the world to attention.

Then, looking up to the heavens, he belted out *'Morning Has Broken'* with such gusto that his delighted patron had to muffle his ears.

When Ryan set him down at the end of the song, Ken trotted over to the tire trough for a drink. He drank, raising his head to the skies with each gulp. Before lowering his head for the next sip, he tilted his head to watch in fascination the planes that had taken off from the nearby Baltimore airport glide across the sky, trailing vapor trails.

After quenching his thirst, he followed his peers and his siblings far afield searching for tasty morsels of fresh earthworms in the meadow. It was not an inordinately difficult task, as the unwise prey lay voluntarily exposed, sunning themselves on grassless patches. When he had had his fill, he left the group and came back to the tire trough by the shack for another drink of water.

Finally, fully sated, Ken ambled over to the

fence to look for Helen.

But she was nowhere to be seen. Nor were the rest of her group anywhere to be found. The pond was deserted.

He even stuck his neck out through the fence, craning it to the left and to the right, to catch a glimpse of Helen. But there was no sign of her. Crestfallen he trudged back to rejoin his team. He felt guilty about having dawdled over his extended breakfast. Helen's absence was an unanticipated disappointment.

As he passed the shack, he ran into Ma, just emerging from the shack after laying her daily brown egg.

"What's the matter, Ken?" she enquired with maternal concern. "Why, you look downright dejected!"

"No ... it's nothing. Everything's fine," mumbled Ken unconvincingly.

"Has it got anything to do with your new friend?" Ma asked gently.

Ken gave a start. His blushed, his comb turning a deep scarlet, as he asked incredulously, "How did you know, Ma?"

Ma smiled enigmatically. "Never forget, I'm your mother. Mothers just know."

Ken shook his head in disbelief as he stumbled away in search of his pals.

It was later in the day, when the sun was half way down to the west, that Ken heard Helen's call. He was in the middle of a friendly joust with his brother and best friend Joey. The two had marked off ten paces and were about to charge at each other in a mock duel with their manes flared. Joey's growls died in his throat when he saw, to his utter surprise, Ken sprint away in the direction of the shack with a hasty, "Excuse me!" Joey was too stunned to give chase.

There was Helen, on the other side of the fence. She had come straight from a dip in the pond. Her damp brown feathers glistened in the afternoon sun.

"Where did you disappear?" Ken asked petulantly, out of breath from his non-stop run to the fence.

"Sorry! We left early this morning."

"*Left early this morning?*" Ken was outraged. "Why didn't you let me know?" Ken asked peevishly.

"Hey! Take it easy now! No reason for you to be upset, eh? We both have our own lives, don't we?" Helen was miffed.

"Sorry, I didn't mean it that way," Ken apologized.

"We left a little after daybreak. I looked for you. You were not near the fence. You must have been at breakfast. There was no way I could've informed you, even if I wanted to. Sorry."

"No worries," Ken relented.

"It's funny, you know. Americans think 'sorry' is solely a Canadian prerogative. As if only Canadians needed to be polite and considerate!" scoffed Helen.

"Where did you go, if I may ask?" Ken was curious.

"You didn't think we had gone back to Canada, did you, eh?" asked Helen with a smile. "Our leader suggested last evening at the debrief meeting that we taper off slowly after the exertions of the long flight here. We will do a few more sorties over the next few days. Today we flew out to the Bay Bridge on the Eastern Shore. It's beautiful."

"Is Canada more beautiful than here?" asked Ken.

"Canada is incredibly beautiful..." began Helen.

Just then, there was a ping as a rock hit the metal fence and ricocheted off in Helen's direction. Helen quickly ducked for cover and the stone whizzed past her head. Before she and Ken could collect their wits, another stone came their way, again narrowly missing Helen. Startled, they both took to the air, fleeing in different directions, making loud agitated noises. Ken's group by the farm house and Helen's compeers near the pond took up the refrain. Above the honking and the cackling came the sound of maniacal laughter from near the house.

"Silly goose!" They heard the young man mock before slamming the door shut.

For a little longer Ken and Helen continued to stalk around warily, continuing to make distress calls, but less stridently than before. When they were satisfied that the danger was past, they got together again by the fence.

"Who was that ruffian?" Helen made no attempt to hide her anger.

"He's Dennis. The elder son. A ne'er do well ... a total loser." Ken spat contemptuously. "He thinks it's a joke to hurt animals. He's an idiot."

"I know the type," said Helen wearily.

"Once when he was either drunk or high on drugs, I don't know which, he came out with a gun and started taking potshots at the cows grazing in the field. His father, Patrick McGuire, the farmer, came running out and snatched the gun from his hands. The father was livid."

"I don't want to hear more about him." Helen said abruptly. "I hate guns and idiots. If there is one thing worse than a fool, it is a fool with a gun. Guns make fools of even the wise. And sadly, there's a surfeit of them in the world."

"The rest of the family are nice. The best is Ryan, the youngest child. The middle one, the daughter, Clara, is a dreamer who lives in her own world. But tell me about Canada and your trip here."

"You seemed a little embarrassed yesterday about being a local. Don't be. Your town, Greenbelt, is my second favorite place in the world. I spend half my time here."

"Really?"

"Yes. Me and my group, we spend half the year in St. Catharines and the other half here in Greenbelt."

"Then you are practically my fellow native! Will you come back again next year?" Ken asked.

"Yes, of course, we will! Come to think of it, I will spend half my life here. Can you imagine? Half my entire life!"

"You all come back every year?"

"Yes, we do. At least most of us do. In the past, everyone did. As a matter of fact, this is my second trip here."

Ken visibly brightened with excitement. "I was born this year. Must have been after you returned to Canada from your first trip. Or I was too small to know. I envy you. You have seen the world at such an early age."

"Actually, migration is no joyride. I will tell you more about it later. I am sorry there has to be this fence between us. Why don't you hop over to this side?" suggested Helen.

"I have never left the farm. And I can't fly. Ma warned us about the dangers that lie beyond the fence," Ken said resignedly.

Helen looked at Ken quizzically. "But outside the fence lie opportunities as well, not just danger," Helen said with a smile. "This whole world is full of walls and fences, some visible, others invisible. If it were not for that frightful devil who chucked rocks at us, I'd come over to your side in a heartbeat."

"I don't think Dennis will come back today. He rarely steps out of the house when the sun's up. He's a crazy night owl. Ma calls him a fiend. Come on over."

"No, not today. I will come another time. Isn't it strange that we are neighbors for half the year? Sounds crazy, eh?"

Ken found this difficult to fathom. "Doesn't it confuse you? To spend half the year there in St. Catharines and the other half here in Greenbelt?"

Helen only smiled, shrugging her shoulders.

"Where do you actually belong?" persisted Ken.

"I don't know. Never really thought about it. I told you yesterday that I'm neither an expat nor a refugee. I think I'm a gypsy. We could be called displaced persons, I suppose. Not refugees. No, definitely not refugees. We don't come here begging for help. Nor do we take what is not ours. And we have no plans to settle down here permanently. We're voluntarily displaced. And that too temporarily."

Helen paused in thought before continuing. "This world, this life, is all temporary. We have no continuing city here. I guess I will be a displaced person all my life."

"I'm sorry ..." began Ken apologetically.

"You're turning Canadian now, eh?" Helen laughed her tinkling laugh. "Don't apologize. I'm not unhappy being a wanderer and wayfarer. I may not have a place to call my home, but that's OK. On the bright side, I'm not burdened by a misguided sense of patriotism for any one country!"

"Never saw it that way. Continuing city, that's a beautiful phrase!" Ken exclaimed.

"It's borrowed from the Book. Not mine. Yes, I have no continuing city. Hmmm ... Come to think of it, no one has. We are all just passing through. All of us are refugees scrambling to live a good life, to make ends meet. We are all of us transients and renters. How long are our lives anyway? Man's three score and ten is still evanescence—not permanence. Not even close!"

"You make a good case, pro detachment and con avarice," Ken said meditatively.

"I don't have a place to call home, but in a way, I belong to the whole world. I'm a Mongolian nomad without a ger! I'm a stateless citizen of the world!" said Helen giggling at the incongruity.

"What's a ger now?" asked Ken perplexed.

"It's like a Kyrgyz yurt." Seeing Ken's puzzled squint, she added, "It's a movable home. How do I explain it? ... Here, I got it! It is like the rusty RV over there in the front yard! Except it doesn't need an engine or use gasoline to pollute the earth."

Ken marveled at Helen's knowledge.

"How do you know all this stuff, about gers and yurts and Mongolia and Kyrgyzstan?" Ken could not hide his amazement.

"Ken, it is nothing supernatural. One has only to remain connected to the Universe. To the cosmic grapevine of knowledge. The vast majority of all creation—Man included—lead disconnected lives. There is this vast body of universal knowledge, understanding, history, and intuition that is there for the asking. For everyone."

"For free?"

"Yes, for free. There is no cost to it. The cosmic connection that we are blessed with at birth gets eroded and fainter with each passing day. Every mundane experience—like fighting for food—severs another tenuous strand of the silver cord, until at last we are unmoored, ignorant and disoriented."

"That's not easy for me to get my head around. Everything I know, I learned from my Ma. She taught me everything. How did you get here from Canada?" Ken was curious.

"We took the usual flyway. Flyways are similar to Man's highways—except there are no tolls," said Helen smiling mischievously.

"You mean something like the Baltimore-Washington Parkway over there or the Beltway?"

"Something like that. Only much broader and higher. And less gridlock too, eh?" Helen smiled again impishly. "We are old school. We belong to the Eastern Tradition," she added enigmatically. "We take the Eastern Atlantic flyway to get here in the fall and for the return trip when spring comes around. There are others further west who take the Mississippi, the Rocky Mountain, or the Pacific flyways."

"Are all the ways or routes the same?" asked Ken.

"Most certainly not! If that were true there would neither be any culs-de-sac nor any roundabouts, would there?"

"Fascinating! Well said!" gushed Ken. "How does it look like from up there when you are flying?"

"We fly high, so high, that rivers look like shimmering ribbons below. And, from above, cars look like moving matchboxes. We try to avoid the broiling, polluted air rising from cities."

"How high do you fly?" Ken could not contain his curiosity.

"We fly high. Usually four to five thousand

feet. Some daredevils go as high as twenty thousand feet."

Ken listened riveted. Finally, he asked.

"Do you fly nonstop?"

"No!" laughed Helen. "It's too far to do that. Nearly a thousand miles. We have pit stops. We break journey at staging posts on the way."

"Food swamps?" queried Ken.

"No! Our staging posts are nothing like the rest stops on Man's highways or freeways. We eat healthy even when we are on the road, or, rather, in the sky."

"The view must be beautiful from up there?"

"Most of the time it is. But there are also large stretches of ugliness created by Man."

"You mean cities?" asked Ken.

"No, not just cities. Man is a selfish, greedy creature. They pillage and loot the environment. You should see what mountaintop mining has done to the land. They have lopped off the entire tops of hills and mountains. Between the fracking and mountaintop mining they are digging themselves into a hole."

"I thought they cared for the environment?"

"There are those who do. But they are a small

minority. The majority are the enemies of the flora and fauna of the world. Yes, enemies. They are mindless of the voiceless screams of the trees they mow down by the acre every minute—yes, every minute—in the Amazon and in Asia. Drilling and mining have turned crystal clear streams into rivers of blood everywhere."

"That's so sad." The information depressed Ken.

"They are chopping the very branch they are sitting on, eh, blissfully oblivious of their imminent destruction. They will take us down with them?"

"Don't those who know protest?" asked Ken.

"The pillagers hide their evil deeds behind high fences and security guards and shameless lies. But it is all laid bare to us feathered folk who travel the skies. Nothing is hidden from the heavens."

"I thought of Man as a demigod," Ken remarked.

"Bah! Far from it. Anyway, enough whining. Not all of them are wicked There are nice ones still left on this planet. Not very far from here in Pennsylvania live the Amish tribe."

"How are they better?"

"The Amish live in near perfect harmony with nature. They wake up with the dawn and retire with the dusk. They don't use machines and fossil fuels. They are completely organic, like us. They are more akin to us than any other people on earth. Margaret—our leader—has chosen Amish territories for all three of our staging posts. You said you don't fly. Might I ask why?"

"Why don't I fly? Are you serious? We chicken, we don't fly like you. That's why. We are creatures of the earth—not of the air," Ken said defensively.

"But, you and I, we are members of the same bird family!" exclaimed Helen. "We are both birds! Some foolish forebear of yours decided to take the low road. Sorry for the pun. You should reclaim your birthright," Helen suggested.

Ken laughed. "No thanks! I don't think I can ever fly."

"That's not true. You flew when that devil— what's his name—pelted stones at us."

"That was involuntary. Out of fear. And for less than a minute. It can hardly be called flying. More like fleeing, that was."

"The point is—you *could* fly, if you tried. If you can fly for a minute you can fly for an hour!"

"But I don't *want* to fly!" Ken was adamant.

"OK. No pressure. You have free will. We all do. But don't completely discount what I said. Just think about it. On a different note. You know something? You sing beautifully."

Ken blushed for the second time in a day. His comb flushed a deep beet.

Helen continued. "You do. I heard you sing this morning as we were taking off. Will you sing me a song before I go?"

Ken was suddenly self-conscious. But he knew this was his chance to impress Helen.

He cleared his throat nervously several times before breaking out into 'This Land Is Your Land.'

Helen did not hide her delight. When he was done singing, she clapped her wings in applause.

"You are the handsome chanticleer—right out of Chaucer!"

"Thank you!" Ken blushed a third time.

Ken was ecstatic. He did not know who Chaucer was but what did he care!

Not to be outdone, Helen burst into song also, taking Ken by surprise. She sang the Canadian version of 'This Land Is Your Land' in a melodious, mezzo-soprano voice.

Ken applauded enthusiastically.

"Many thanks for the song! You sing beautifully too!"

"Merci. But it's time for me to go. See you tomorrow!" With that Helen was airborne and headed for the pond.

## 3 THE MIGRANT COMES A-CALLING

Helen alighted, as promised, on Ken's side of the fence the next morning. Ken admired the grace of her landing, leaning ever so slightly back as she neared the ground, feet thrust forward, arms open wide.

"Welcome to my humble abode! Won't you come on in?" Ken crooned, beaming. He was all puffed up to have this beautiful exotic female guest come visiting.

A small group of his tribe that was some distance away perked up at the sight of the caller. They raised their heads to gawk at the foreigner and tittered.

Ken looked around. He needed his mother. But she was not in the group of onlookers. 'Now, where did she go? Is she still in the shack laying the daily egg or is she over on the other side where the hay bales are?' wondered Ken.

He felt suddenly unsure about what to do next. "Would you like to go indoors?" offered Ken.

Helen hesitated. "No ... I don't think so. I think I'll pass. It is not that I don't trust you, Ken, but who knows about the others on the farm, especially that evil human, Dennis?"

Sensing Ken's embarrassment at the refusal, she added. "Moreover, I'm claustrophobic. I'm an outdoors girl. All of us Canada geese are. Let's just stay out and enjoy the sun, eh?"

Ken found his voice. "Dennis is the very opposite of you. He is agoraphobic. He hardly ever steps out of the house. Usually it is only to meet shady characters for drug deals after dark. Yesterday was one of those rare occasions when he stepped out during daylight hours. Not that I'm complaining. I get no pleasure out of seeing his ugly, evil face."

Helen looked at him thoughtfully.

"Do you have any idea how lucky you are to be here?" Helen asked surveying the farm.

"Me, lucky? Why would you say that? I never considered myself particularly fortunate to be here," Ken responded doubtfully.

"Do you realize what a huge blessing loose

housing, as it is called, is? Your group is a privileged lot—one in a million, nay more than a million—to have both the freedom to roam around and a roof above your head to protect you from the elements and enemies. The majority of your kind—I'd safely guess ninety-nine percent—are cooped up in cages all their life. Some of them are so cramped up, they can barely stand upright, let alone flex their limbs. There's bullying and gangsterism and every other bad thing that happens in prisons. And they are slaughtered in their prime, if one can call it prime in such dismal conditions. Not a single moment of happiness from birth in serfdom till painful execution while still in captivity. Mass killing, actually. You are lucky. Very, very, very, very lucky."

"How terrible that life must be! How dreadful the slavery! Ma told us about farm-bondage, but she did not go into graphic details. What you narrate is shocking. You know, you have more freedom than anyone. I envy you your liberty, Helen."

"Sure, we have our freedom. And I wouldn't trade it for anything in this world. But, unlike you, we sometimes don't know where our next meal is coming from. Plus, living in the wild does not always make happy campers on account of the vagaries of the weather. We are encompassed by sworn enemies who'd like nothing better than to tear us from limb to limb or devour us whole. You have the best of both worlds. Freedom—if somewhat limited—and assured creature comforts and security. What more would anyone ask for, eh?"

Ken thought about all this for a moment.

"I never gave all this much thought before. But I always yearned for a life of complete and unfettered freedom. To see the amazing world that Ma tells us about."

"That's not a bad goal to have, to see the world. And if you want it badly enough, you will get your wish someday soon."

"Me see the world? Not a chance!" Ken pooh-poohed the idea.

"Why is the place so quiet?" asked Helen nodding her head in the direction of the house.

"They have all gone to church. All except the nut case. Ma told me he sleeps during the day and plays video games all night. He's as crazy as a loon!"

"Now, now," remonstrated Helen, "don't go stereotyping our cousins! Loons are perfectly sane compared to humans."

She stopped suddenly to laugh when she saw the irony.

"I can't believe I'm defending loons! The loon is the arch rival of the Canada goose for the honor of the national bird of Canada."

"But you bear the name of your country!" pointed out Ken. "Your tribe deserves it more than anyone else. Ma thinks the world of you."

"Your mother is kind. If it's meant to be, we will be chosen as Canada's national bird. We may not win, though. There is a lobby that holds our annual migration and absence from the country against us," Helen said shrugging her shoulders.

"Really? How is international travel a disqualifier? You are not renouncing your citizenship. You are only traveling," argued Ken.

"Man's politics is complicated. Thankfully we don't set much store by Man's honors," Helen replied disdainfully.

"But an honor ..." began Ken.

"It is better—better by far—to attain all that the Creator fashioned us to be. That's what is of greater importance," Helen stated with conviction.

Ken's thoughts were elsewhere. "Do you see the coincidence? You are a national bird and I'm a state bird. No prizes for guessing which state since we are Rhode Island Reds," Ken said with a wry smile. "Ma told us there are even two competing monuments in honor of my tribe in the state of Rhode Island, one at Adamsville and the other at Little Compton. Well, I hope you beat the loons and get to be the national bird."

"By the way, Canadians call their currency the loon, which, in my opinion, is a little loony, eh?"

"Ha, ha. They could hardly have called it the goose, could they?" laughed Ken.

Helen changed tack. "You know, your tribe has done very well for foreigners," Helen said with a glint in her eye.

Ken knew what she was getting at. "We don't talk about that part of our history much. We consider ourselves natives, and all who come after us encroachers and refugees. Ma told me that our forefathers came from the Malay peninsula in South-East Asia. We have lost our heritage and language and forgotten all our customs and our own way of life. We are solid American Rhode Island Reds now."

"I recommend exploring your roots. Reclaim your heritage. To do that, tap deeper into the Cosmos. You will reconnect with your country cousins wherever they are and regain your lost birthright, paternal and maternal," Helen suggested.

"Yes, I have been yearning to follow my ancestors. Need to talk to my uncles about it. But I don't think they will be excited. They are a bunch of grubby freeloaders," Ken said morosely.

"What about your father?" asked Helen and right away she regretted having asked that question.

Ken's eyes welled with tears. "They killed him when I was just two months. The cannibals cooked him for Maggie's birthday and ate him." The grief was still fresh in his mind. "They slit his neck behind the kitchen right in front of all of us."

"Sorry," whispered Helen. She said it with such empathy that it was a balm for the reopened wound.

Ken muttered a choked word of thanks. Shared sorrow drew them closer together.

Before she returned to her flock, she brought up the subject of flight again.

"You should fly," she said casually, as she flexed her wings for the flight back to her flock.

Then she added decisively.

"After hearing your story today, I feel all the more strongly that your salvation lies in flying."

Ken was about to protest but thought the

better of it.

"Have a bite before you go," invited Ken.

"I'm not sure. Not really peckish right now. Is that chicken feed from the factories?" asked Helen doubtfully.

"No, it's corn."

"OK, grains are fine. I hope it's not indoors?" Helen still hesitated.

"No, it is by the water-trough on the other side of the shack," answered Helen.

They strolled over to Ken's breakfast spot where he had saved half his breakfast for Helen. Ken was happy just watching Helen eat. He himself only took a peck or two. He marveled at Helen's unhurried, prim manner of dining—the complete antithesis of his comrades. When the corn was all gone, they moved to the trough to drink.

As usual, Ken watched the airplanes zipping across the sky as he ingested the water. Helen instead looked closely at the ominous gray clouds.

"Looks like there will be snow tonight," Helen observed. Ken did not seem to hear.

In between sips, he asked.

"You know what I have always wondered? How does a corn seed know to sprout as corn and a maize seed as maize?"

"Ha, ha, ha. They are both the same, silly! Just different names," laughed Helen.

Ken smiled sheepishly. "OK, OK. How about corn and wheat then?"

"I don't know, Ken. I have wondered about this myself. The Creator made them all. Just look at ourselves. Our eyes, beaks, the plumes, to say nothing of all the complicated stuff within—heart, lungs, stomach, and all the other innards. We are fearfully and wonderfully made. How can Man believe it all just came together out of thin air? It is monstrously ludicrous."

"You mean, Man thinks everything just happened out of nothing?" Ken was incredulous.

"Yes, they think there was a loud bang and every living thing just popped up alive and perfectly made and continue to upgrade themselves with each passing year," Helen smile was condescending.

"They are stupider than I thought! What are we? Self-creating automobile models?" Ken gasped.

"Do you eat processed chicken feed sometimes?" asked Helen.

"No, farmer Patrick is a reformed hippie from

the 70s. He listens to the Beatles, Creedence Clearwater Revival, the Seekers, and the Monkees, and a lot of Sinatra, all the time. He is liberal and progressive. Very, laissez-faire, actually. He prefers everything organic. That's how we got to be free-range, Ma told me," explained Ken.

"You are lucky. Stick to the grains that Ryan feeds you and to greens you can forage on your own. Starve if you must, but don't go anywhere near the factory-made stuff. It contains the blood and flesh of cows and pigs and, sorry to make your stomach turn, even your very own kind."

"Eww! How gross!" said Ken grimacing in disgust.

"Do you eat only corn then?" asked Helen.

"No! Of course, not! Who could live only on corn? We scour the fields for the juiciest worms and insects ..."

"Yuck! Stop! Don't go on. I thought your diet was more refined than that of your compatriots," Helen said making a face.

"And what do *you* eat?" asked Ken stung to the quick.

"We are pacifists. Sure, our males are agonistic. But only when they defend their families against marauders. We do not kill other living beings for pleasure or for food. We graze the open fields. We are herbivores. We eat grass, leaves, seeds and grains, berries, and also algae and plankton in the water."

"But aren't plants living beings too?" countered Ken.

"You have a point. Yes, they are. But if one were to eat nothing at all, how would one survive? We would all starve to death. Our vegan diet is the most humane there can be. The seeds and grain we eat are not killed. They are transmitted. And the leaves and stems would have fallen any way. We play our role in fertilizing the plants for growth—not death."

"Your vegan diet gives you the strength to fly hundreds of miles?" asked Ken.

"Of course! Meat is grossly overrated. Grain and greens. That's the mantra for good health! You haven't seen many humans. If you did you would be surprised at the sizes of some them. Elephantoid! Mammoth!"

"Is it right to mock their disease?" queried Ken hesitantly.

"*Disease?* Pshaw! Gluttony is a sin - not a disease. Same with perversion. Or addiction. Or alcoholism. Man tries to wriggle out of their shortcomings by shifting blame. What better way to avoid owning responsibility than laying the blame at the doorstep of microbes or chemicals and calling it an ailment!"

"Is that really true?"

"Of course, it is! They just have to man up instead of sniveling like sissies. Most humans are unaware of the enormous strength of the will power they are blessed with. They don't even know they have it. They grovel through life like weaklings instead of walking tall."

"What makes them so fat?"

"Their craving for food has destroyed their health. People of wealthier countries are half as much bigger than those of poorer nations. It has come to such a state that you can gauge a national wealth by looking at the people's girth. Your country has the most obese people in the world. Mine is slightly better. We have our fat ones too. But the percentage of the corpulent and the stout among humans is astoundingly high."

It was soon time to part.

"I had better be going. Thanks for the meal and the chat," Helen said graciously.

"You are welcome. Any time! By the way, I

spoke to Ma about connecting to the wisdom and knowledge repository of the Universe. She said I was old enough to have a link of my own. She added, I was the only one to ask for this. We pullets have such short life spans. Expanding our knowledge is the least of our worries."

"That is very good news that you have the permission! Your mother is one in a million!"

"Yes, she is. You know what Ma said? She made an interesting comment. She said the future lay in the past."

"Your mother is a very wise lady. All the wisdom that we would ever need was given to our forefathers. There is nothing new under the sun. Make the most of your new resource."

"I will."

Helen rose at a steep angle to clear the fence before gliding down to the pond at the lower level on the other side.

After Helen had left, Ken began to seriously ponder about changing his dietary habits—and about flying.

+++

As Helen had predicted, the snow came down that night. By morning the whole area resembled an enormous frosted cake. Snow covered the ground and the roofs of the house, the shed, and the shack. The snow on the drooping branches made the trees look like stooping old men, somber, white-haired. The sky was dark and steely gray. Even the smoke was loath to leave the warmth of the chimney, hovering over it like a pall, instead of joyously floating up to the blue skies on a summer's day.

There was no let-up. It continued to snow all through the day. The temperature plummeted rapidly. It was freezing cold even indoors. But, mercifully, Ryan did not forget them in the shed. He strung an extension cord from the kitchen and brought in a space heater to warm their shack. He fed them corn till they were sated and brought in warm water for them to drink.

In spite of all this, it was not easy to stay confined with a restless, fidgety bunch. There was shoving and pushing for vantage positions around the space heater. Fights broke out between the young roosters.

Ken played it safe and stuck close to his mother. Even in the midst of the jostling crowd, she did not lose her poise. No wonder, the clan always treated her with the utmost respect.

When night fell, fierce winds lashed the shack. The whistling gusts terrified even the elders. The temperature plunged still further. They all huddled closer to each other as they tried to sleep in the orange-red glow of the electric heater.

Ken thought often about Helen in the cold outdoors.

"How will the visitors survive?" he asked Ma.

"They were made for weather like this. It is not a huge problem for them. They will be just fine. Don't worry about your friend. You will meet her when the snow stops."

But the snow did not stop falling that night.

The next day was even worse. By morning, the snow changed to sleet and hail. The pounding on the roof together with the stifling stench of the confined space made the situation almost unbearable.

Ken began to wilt.

Ma was supportive. "Don't let yourself be beaten by this situation. There are tougher battles to be fought in life. Just think of the visitors out in the open."

That night it was quiet again as it was before the storm. The howling wind had passed over Greenbelt on its way south. The snow, sleet, and hail capitulated and retreated along with the wind.

The next morning, the whole group rushed out en masse. The air smelt pure and clean. The cloudless sky was a deep blue against the white of the snow-clad earth. The gray smoke spiraled up straight, thinning as it climbed higher and higher.

Ken let the stampede precede him. When he stepped out, he was almost blinded by the bright sun. He gulped in lungfuls of fresh air. The water in the tire trough had frozen solid. Ryan brought hot water in a kettle. As his patron poured the steaming water into the trough, Ken sang. His rendition of 'Morning Has Broken' was truly heartfelt. All was well with the world again.

Ken hurried over to the fence. He did not have to wait long. Helen who was looking up from the banks of the pond took off directly and alighted on the other side.

"How have you been?" Helen asked gaily.

Ken marveled at her appearance. She looked so bright and cheerful that the snow storm just past could have been mistaken for a visit to the spa.

"I'm OK. But it was terrible indoors," replied Ken.

"My, you look so bedraggled!"

"Believe you me, it is not easy to spend three

whole days and nights indoors with a group like mine. I have the worst case of cabin fever. Look at you! You look none the worse for wear ... or, rather, the weather. How do you manage to pull it off?"

"We must give nature it's due. Roll with the punches, so to speak. You like blue skies and balmy weather, eh?" asked Helen with a twinkle in her eye.

"Yes, of course! Who doesn't? I hate snow, rain, and sleet. And I hate wind, thunder, and lightning too!" Ken said emphatically.

"They are all good for us," was Helen's quiet response.

"Good for us? That I find very hard to believe. How can harsh weather be good for anyone?" Ken asked disbelievingly.

"Just think for a moment, Ken," reasoned Helen gently, "where would we be without the rains and thunderstorms? We'd be pushing up the daisies! We'd all be dead!"

Seeing the uncomprehending look on Ken's face, she continued.

"Yes, if it were just blue skies all the time, we would all be extinct. All living things. We'd be as dead as dodos."

Helen paused before continuing. Ken did not get it.

"Without the rain where would plants and trees get water from? There would be no fruits or flowers. Without lightning and thunder how would nitrogen be fixed, and the land be fertile? If we had no winter at all in the north, the southern hemisphere would become one huge glacier park."

A look of comprehension dawned on Ken's face.

"I now see what you are saying," Ken said with a smile.

"That's why I thank the Creator for rainy days, for lightning and thunder, for snow and ice … for everything that comes our way. Each of them has a purpose. The difficult and the easy. The good and the bad. They are all part of the grand design."

"I never thought of the weather this way before," Ken said thoughtfully.

"There is one more thing that we must always remember. It rains alike on the just and the unjust," said Helen.

A thought struck Ken.

"What are you smiling at?" asked Helen.

"I just realized another reason for me to love icy cold winter," Ken said with an impish smile.

"What's that?" asked Helen frowning.

"If it were not for the winter you would not have come here, and I would never have got to meet you!" Ken grinned.

Helen blushed and pretended to be irritated.

"Stop that nonsense. I have to get back to my team. We are going afield for food today. By the way, have you given any further thought to flying?" Helen asked.

"I've thought about it a few times, but it does seem such an impossibility," Ken said resignedly.

Then Helen said something that made time stand still.

"If wingless Man can fly, why can't you? You have wings and feathers. You are a bird. A bird born to fly."

Ken was thunderstruck.

Before he could collect his wits to respond, Helen uttered a cheery, "See you later!"

With that she was gone.

## 4 · Don't Fence Me In

The next time they met, Ken had a request.

"Helen, tell me about your town, St. Catharines."

"Well, what can I say, Canada is Canada, eh!" Helen smiled before continuing. "I love the place. That's where I was born. But as I said already, Greenbelt is as much my home as St. Catharines is."

"But it's not the same, is it?" pressed Ken.

"Well, no. St. Catharines has a feel of its own. It is on the Niagara Peninsula, midway between two of the Great Lakes, Erie and Ontario. It's close to the famous waterfalls. My favorite spots are Port Dalhousie on the Ontario side and Port Colborne on the Erie side."

"Are those lakes much bigger than the pond over there?" asked Ken.

Helen cracked up laughing. But just as quickly she pulled herself together to assume her lady-like mien.

"Pardon me. Didn't mean to offend you. You haven't seen those Great Lakes. If you had, you too would have laughed like I did. They are b-i-g!"

"How big?" Ken persisted.

"So big, you can't see the other side. So big, there are ships bigger than that house over there floating around in them."

"I cannot get my head around that," Ken admitted.

"Your mother must have told you about the famous Niagara Falls?"

Ken nodded.

"We go there at least once every week. Our other haunts are Welland and Thorold, especially the quiet Gibson Lake between them. The Montebello Park with the roses is beautiful but with no waterhole it is not goose friendly. We circle over it admiring the roses."

"Other than lakes, what does St. Catharines have that Greenbelt doesn't?"

"The opposite is easier. I know what Greenbelt has, that St. Catharines does not have. Guns. A lot of them. Americans are gun crazy, eh?"

"Farmer Patrick has a gun too. That was what Dennis used to fire at the cows with."

"Hey, I just thought of the Niagara escarpment. All nature. That area is also called the Greenbelt. What a coincidence! There you go, that's something in common between the two places! There is also history that links Maryland and Ontario. The last stop of Harriet Tubman's Underground Railroad that wound its way through Maryland was St. Catharines, Ontario. Very historic."

"I did not know there was an underground railroad that long," Ken commented doubtfully.

"No! It wasn't a real railroad. That was the name for the escape route to the north that the black slaves took, from one safe house to the next safe house."

"Oh, I hadn't ever heard of that. I will never get to see the Niagara Falls or the Great Lakes," Ken said morosely.

Helen was silent for a minute. Then she said, "What you lose on the swings you gain on the roundabouts."

"What's that supposed to mean?"

"You have the comfort of a home, an assured food supply, and safety and security. I don't have any of those. But instead, I get to see places. It all cancels out. That's universal justice for you, eh."

"I don't know ..." began Ken doubtfully.

"Well, one thing I do know. If one does not aspire for a goal, there is no goal to reach. You need to get started with flying."

"There you go again! Stop nagging me! I've told you umpteen times that I'm a ground bird." Ken was miffed.

Helen decided to ignore the 'nagging' remark.

"What now, a ground bird? That's an absurdity!"

"Helen, the other day you compared me to Man who flies in big airplanes that have frighteningly loud engines. That was an unfair comparison. I don't have jet engines to fly," Ken said peevishly.

"But you have wings! Man doesn't. You're impossible! You won't even try! Mankind made many, many attempts before they could fly. You haven't lifted those wings of yours even a teeny, weeny bit."

"You are the highflying jet setter—I'm just a landlubber," said Ken diffidently.

"Now don't go saying that. There is nothing I disagree with more. Our lineage may be different, but we are both birds. We are of the same family."

"But you can fly, and I cannot," Ken insisted.

"You and your silly excuses! You are a bird, for crying out loud! Just like us. You were born to fly! You need to fly! You can fly, if only you tried!" Helen egged Ken on.

"You don't convince me one bit," Ken said adamantly.

"You have two wings! What are wings for, if not for flying? You were created to fly. The Creator did not make you a crawling snake. You are a bird that can fly. For whatever reason, your ancestors gave up flying. Now's your chance to claim it back. To be all that you were meant to be. To fly. Don't accept the status quo. Break the shackles of slavery. Discover yourself. Throw caution to the winds. Fly in the face of presumption," urged Helen.

All to no avail.

Ken would not be moved.

But after Helen had left Ken flexed his wings. He recalled his brief flight when Dennis had chucked stones at Helen. This time there was no imminent danger to flee from. Without much effort, he flew in a straight line, a few feet above the ground, all the way to the doorstep of his shack.

+++

Some days later Helen surprised him with an invitation.

"Come on over and meet my folks."

"Meet your folks? They are out by the lake and I'm here inside the fence."

"It's only this fence that you have to clear," Helen countered. "I've been giving you broad hints about your innate flying ability. You have not only not made a single attempt, but you also refuse even to mentally consider the possibility."

Ken remained silent. Helen continued.

"All this talk of flying—all this theory—this second-hand talk—will do you no good unless you stretch out those Creator-given wings of yours and take flight and soar."

"No, I am sure I can't," Ken said weakly.

A quaver crept into his voice when he thought of the dread of flying high and then falling to the earth in a heap.

"I'm positive you can. You've never tried. That's all. Let me tell you a story that Mom told me when I was young, and I was faced with many self-doubts and infirmities."

"A true story?" asked Ken a little skeptically.

"Yes, a true story. Wilma was born prematurely to poor black parents who couldn't afford to bring up a girl child. To make matters worse, as a child she was afflicted with polio and became paralyzed. But her mother never gave up. Wilma too gave it all she had. That Wilma, who was once lame and crippled, became the fastest woman on earth and won the Olympic gold when she was twenty. Some turnaround, eh?"

"I thought you were going to tell me a true story. You are kidding, right?"

"I'm not making this up! It really did happen."

"OK, I believe you, if you say so. You are not one for telling lies. Determination trumps improbability?" queried Ken.

Helen pressed home the advantage.

"Now, if a polio-stricken Wilma Rudolph can become the fastest woman sprinter in the world—with an Olympic gold to show for it—what is it that perfectly healthy, well-bodied individuals like you and me cannot do? Come on, give it a shot!"

"OK. You win! I will attempt to jump the fence."

"That's the spirit! You can do it! I'll go ahead and wait for you on the other side."

Helen waved her wings to gently rise, almost in slow motion, over the fence to the other side.

Ken decided it was now or never.

He flailed his wings and with a strong push took off. But he realized almost immediately that he was going to crash into the chain-link fence. With a desperate left turn, Ken landed unharmed just inside the fence some distance to the left.

Helen, on the other side, scurried to her right to be close to where Ken had made the emergency landing.

"Don't worry. You need a bit more space for the lift. Go further back. You can do it! Go for it!" she goaded him on.

Ken, flushed with adrenaline, ran several paces back and, turning around, took off. This time he cleared the fence with much to spare. The landing was clumsy but that did not matter one bit. They were both over the moon.

"I did it! I jumped over the fence! I'm free!" screamed Ken ecstatically.

"Pipe down! And don't even think of singing a song! The whole world will know what you did."

"OK, I won't sing. But this is wonderful. The grass feels so soft. The air here is so pristine!" said Ken doing a jig.

"There's barely any grass. And it's the very same air. You're only twenty feet from the fence! It's just the feeling of freedom, of unfettered liberty. Keep a lid on it," urged Helen.

But Ken would not be contained.

"I am free! No more fences!" he exulted.

Irrepressible Ken then broke into song. Fittingly, it was 'Don't Fence Me In'. But heeding Helen's warning, he sang sotto voce instead of belting it out.

"You know, Ken, fences are strange things. Once upon a time, the Iron Curtain fenced people in. They wanted to escape from their own countries, but they could not. The guards would shoot them if they tried. When they got their freedom, the walls were torn down. Now the very same people are building new fences to keep refugees out and themselves in. It is the height of irony, don't you think?"

But Ken wasn't listening. He continued to prance around singing. "I'm free! I'm free!"

Ken romped on the sparse grass. He ran this way and that. He ran in circles flapping his wings. He made figure eights, banking his wings like an airplane.

"I hate to bring you down to earth, Ken. This is just a brief outing to meet my people. You are going back over the fence right after."

"Must I? Couldn't I live on my own in the wild like you?" pleaded Ken.

"You are alone and totally unprepared for life on your own. You don't have a clue what's in store for you. There's no way you will be able to survive even for a day. You must go back," Helen said firmly.

After a few more minutes of Ken's caper, Helen said, "We need to get a move on. You can't be AWOL too long."

They started walking together down the gentle slope to the pond.

Suddenly the enormity of what he was about to do hit Ken.

With each step, Ken's discomfiture grew.

Halfway to the pond's edge, he got cold feet. He stopped and turned to Helen.

"Helen, I'm not sure this is ... this is a good ...

a good idea. I think I'll turn ... turn back to the farm," Ken stammered nervously.

"*Turn back?*" Helen was astonished. "What's come over you all of a sudden?"

"I don't know. This is outside my comfort zone. I'm not good at meeting strangers, let alone foreigners. And on top of that, I don't speak your lingo ..." began Ken apologetically.

"We are speaking to each other now, for heaven's sake! We are communicating, aren't we?" Helen could not help letting her exasperation show.

"We are," Ken agreed. "Between us, it's fine. But with your group? They will make fun of my accent. They will mock my appearance. Why do I need this aggravation? Give me one good reason. I'm dead meat!" Ken said despondently.

"So, that's the problem, eh?" Helen said, visibly relaxing. "First off, you have set your hand to the plough. You ought not to turn back. Secondly, you are going to meet fifteen wonderful persons who are close to my heart. They are my family and my relatives," Helen tried to convince Ken.

"But still ..." began Ken.

"As for your accent, Ken, wear it as a symbol

of quiet pride. A badge of courage, so to speak. An accent signifies that the speaker is brave enough to be outside the home turf—to be a minority, an outsider, a johnnie-come-lately, a globetrotting cosmopolitan, an intrepid wayfarer who dreams of a brave new world and has the courage to venture outside of his home in search of it," Helen said emphatically.

Ken could only manage a weak smile.

"Lack of fluency in an unfamiliar language is not an indication of your mental deficiency. Rather, it is an indication that you know the language of the person you are talking to, better than he or she knows yours. The mocker is a coward who lacks the courage to step out of the comfort zone of the language his mother taught him. The boot is, in fact, on the other foot! The scorner is the one to be pitied."

There was a pregnant pause as Ken digested it.

"Look at it this way. The one despising your accent knows little or next to nothing of your language—certainly not enough to speak it— while you are smart enough to converse with him or her in their own tongue. Tell me, who is better off?"

After a brief pause, Helen asked pushing home the advantage. "You know who most certainly does not have an accent?"

"No. Who?" asked Ken.

"A redneck frog-in-the-well, that's who!" Helen smiled broadly. "And you are not that."

Ken could not but grin.

"You know something else? An accent is a pass-along kind of thing. Something like a baton. When you are in my neck of the woods, you have it, and when I'm in your territory, I'm the one holding it. It's a movable thing. It's always about the others—never you. The accent bothers them—not you. And everyone has an accent—if they ever went visiting or socialized."

Ken seemed reassured.

Helen continued. "I'm not suggesting for a moment that one not make efforts to soften a grating accent and speak as close as possible to the natives, but there is no need to be ashamed or apologetic about a lingering vestige of an accent either. And never, ever, be bashful about looking different from others. You are a unique creation of the Creator. You are not of your own making. So, who are you to apologize, eh?"

"I do not disagree with what you say. But meeting a cohort of new people?" Ken was still hesitant.

"You see, like I told you, we fly to Niagara Falls. To Port Dalhousie. To Hamilton. And once we flew even as far as the big city, Toronto, on the other side of Lake Ontario. And we flew via New York state and Pennsylvania to get here. We come across diverse human beings all the time. Some kind, others not so much. We meet other creatures too. I've run into flocks of seagulls, terns, sparrows, and even crows. There's a farm near the Welland Canal where I mingled with horses and cows and pigs."

"My, you do get around!"

"Not as much as I would like," smiled Helen. "When I meet others, I am interested in them— their lives, their stories, their ideas. Not in how they look or how they talk, eh?"

Helen continued after a pause. "Here's my little secret. When it comes to others, I'm color blind and accent deaf. I revel in the commonality, however little, that I see, instead of searching zealously for differences to despise them with."

Ken nodded his head in agreement.

Helen continued.

"If you think about it, there really is no disparity. We are all the same irrespective of our origins. At the same time, each one of us is unique.

That paradox is the key to life."

"You are quite the philosopher!"

Helen went on. "And I have no time to think about my own differences. All my attention is focused on them. Not on me. I am what I am. They are what they are. And together we make this a wonderful world!"

"I envy you, Helen. I want to see the world too!"

"A good place to start would be my tribe. Shall we get on with this visit, eh?" Helen asked with a mischievous smile.

Ken was ready.

Contrary to his apprehensions, the visit turned out to be quite pleasant. They were all by the water's edge. As Ken and Helen got close, the lookout doing guard duty perked up and started honking.

"Hey, Fritz, cut it out. I'm bringing along a friend not a foe," called out Helen.

The whole group drew up in a semi-circle facing Helen and Ken. There were smiles of welcome.

The leader spoke. "Welcome to our group, Ken."

One of the younger ones tittered. The leader gave the errant gander such a stern look that he froze.

The leader continued, "Helen already told us about you. I am Ruth, the first among equals of our group. Not the chief, but the custodian of our sacred tradition."

Ken could not hide his surprise.

"We are happy you could come. Let me do the introductions first. This here's Hoover, the master emeritus," Ruth said, patting the grizzled gander next to her on the shoulder. "This is his tenth trip. He knows the route like the back of his wing. Needless to add, I value his advice immensely."

Hoover smiled kindly at Ken who nodded respectfully. Ruth continued.

"Hoover's wife Suzie is on her ninth trip. For my husband Peter and I, it is our eighth visit. Next, we have Sasha and Liza on their seventh trip, followed by Fritz and Julie on their fourth pilgrimage. The second-timers are Charlie, Emily, and, your friend, Helen. And lastly, Nancy, Judy, Bruce, and Daniel are the newbies on their maiden voyage"

Hoover leaned over to whisper something to

Ruth.

"I've done it again. I have inadvertently left out Larry, the lone star," said Ruth pointing to a forlorn figure standing at the edge of the water some distance away staring at the horizon. Ruth seemed about to say something more but then shrugged and remained silent.

Ken gave a nervous start at Helen's nudge. He got the hint, clearing his throat noisily.

"Many firsts for me today. First time out of the farm. First time jumping over the fence. First time giving a speech. Maybe if I stayed home, I wouldn't have to be giving speeches," he said with a twinkle in his eyes. The audience laughed. The conversation flowed smoothly with neither any impediments of self-consciousness nor concealed loathing. Ken's misgivings about his accent were misplaced. Nobody gave any indication that he spoke funny.

"We won't burden you with long speeches. We are quite informal that way. We are glad you came. Come again any time," affirmed Ruth.

When the meeting was over, and Helen's compatriots gathered around for chats with Ken, Helen intervened saying, "Ken has to get back to his farm. He will be in trouble if he does not return soon."

And then to Ken she offered, "Come, I will walk you to the fence."

When they were out of earshot of the group, Ken said, "I have a thousand questions that I am dying to ask. But I will hold off for now. Need to get back to home base."

From that day forth, it was almost always Ken who crossed over to meet Helen, except on rare occasions when Helen cleared the boundary in the opposite direction.

## 5  DEFYING GRAVITY

It was a mild winter's day. Cold, but above freezing. The sun shone blindingly bright through the leafless branches etched against the blue sky. A few white clouds sailed languidly under the green waters of the pond.

Ken could hardly contain himself. He vaulted over the chain-link fence to join Helen beneath the oak tree, not far from the farm boundary.

"I cannot hold my questions in any longer," he announced. "But before I ask them, I just want to say how much I enjoyed meeting your team. Thank you for receiving me so warmly."

"You're welcome, Ken. You weren't the only one who benefitted. Now that my team knows who I'm hobnobbing with, they don't worry anymore."

"Great! Here's my first question. Your leader is a female. Isn't that unusual?"

"No, not for us Canada geese. Our leaders are always female. We are matriarchal! In this respect, we are a bit like the matrilineal Khasi tribe of the Indian state of Meghalaya. It is a goose that leads us on our migrations—not a gander."

Ken stared at Helen open-mouthed.

Ruth smiled. "It is not because males don't like asking for directions. I know what you are thinking. It is unheard of in your patriarchal society. Roosters rule the roost, right? Sorry to be blunt, and I won't say more, but hens in your tribe are only a little better than second-class citizens. We are different. We look up to our females for leadership. Not that we ignore our males. The ganders have their place too. As I told you before, they are agonistic and fierce protectors of their families. They love their children so much that they also participate in child rearing. Our family ties are very strong."

"Wow! You are a progressive tribe way ahead of others and the times!" Ken said in admiration.

"Actually, we have been this way from time immemorial. Our values are ageless and immutable. We think it illogical to consider one gender superior to the other. Both have their own roles and are complementary. How could we survive and propagate without both genders? What was your second question now?"

"What about your leaders?" asked Ken.

"In the realm of égalité, the French could take a leaf out of our books. There are no blue bloods in our midst. All our blood runs uniformly red. We have no kings or queens. No dukes or duchesses. No counts or countesses. And no dictators—benevolent or otherwise."

"What's with Larry? Was he displeased to meet me? Is he a xenophobe? He didn't come anywhere close. He did not even look in my direction."

"No, it has nothing to do with you. Larry is a loner," said Helen.

"Why is he such a sad sack? Is he a nut case?"

"He is not. He is going through some tough times right now. We will talk about it later. But first, we need to get some flying in, eh?"

Ken's first attempt at flight was a dismal failure, though not a life-threatening catastrophe.

He flew up at a low angle to the lowest branch of the oak tree some distance away without any difficulty. But when he alighted on the limb, he could barely hold on to it for dear life. His heart pounded like a jackhammer in his chest as he struggled to get a footing. He was only about eight feet from the ground but to the debutant flier it seemed ten times that.

"Good! Go up higher! Higher!" yelled Helen from below.

Ken did not pay any heed to Helen's words. He wanted to get it over with. If he waited any longer, he would have to follow Helen's advice. So instead he jumped.

He jumped before he had pulled himself together. In his haste, his feet slipped on the cold branch and he fell, off-balance and out of control. He plunged straight down, like a deadweight, in free fall, though he quickly came to his senses and began flailing his wings in fear.

But it was too little, too late. Having jumped from a height of only about eight feet, there was not enough leeway for correction. The last-minute frantic wing flapping softened the fall. He hit the ground with a gentle thud, his feet buckling under him, the outstretched wings cushioning the impact.

Helen, all concern, flew to Ken's side.

She was relieved to find that he was all right. Ken attempted a wan smile.

"I goofed. I feel so silly," Ken said sheepishly.

"Au contraire! You may have reason to be happy," was Helen's response.

"Happy? Are you out of your mind? What do you mean?" Ken said irritably.

"Well, look at it this way. Unless you know how not to do it, how can you do it right? Without the disappointment of failure, how you can you savor success? And, unless you have yourself suffered, how can you comfort others, eh?"

"That is all very well for you to say. It is cold comfort to me. As is this ground," Ken said wryly scampering to get up.

"Well?" asked Helen when Ken was back on his feet.

Ken paused flexing his limbs to look at Helen.

"I want to fly!" he said matter-of-factly.

"That's the spirit! Failure is not defeat. Real defeat is giving up and not trying. If you are truly determined to fly, you will fly. Nothing can stop you. Nothing. Got that?"

Ken nodded.

"Pardon the pun, but chickening out is not an option here."

Without further persuasion from Helen, Ken

made a gallant second attempt.

As he prepared, after those words from Helen, the fear of failure returned. A highly-strung Ken took off from the ground to perch again on the low branch.

"You are going to fly now, Ken! You are going to get your wings today!" Helen encouraged him from below.

Ken hesitated. Even from this height Helen looked so much smaller and the ground so far down.

"Up a rung! Go one level higher!" urged Helen.

Adrenaline coursed through Ken's veins. His throat dried up. Like summer rain on the shack's tin-roof, his heart beat a furious tattoo, much as it had done on the first essay.

Helen's words reverberated in his mind: "Failure is not defeat ... real defeat is giving up and not trying ... chickening out is not an option."

Yet, he still hesitated. Then he chided himself. 'Don't disgrace yourself in front of Helen. What's a mere ten more feet anyway? Enough thinking.'

With an ungainly leap, he launched himself upward in a steep climb to a higher branch of the next tree. The landing, just seconds later, was not any the more graceful than the take-off. He scrambled desperately to not fall off the cold, slimy surface.

Ken breathed a sigh of relief when he had steadied himself. Helen, looking up, flapped her wings in encouragement. A sense of attainment, however small, filled his heart. This was the highest he had ever been. He felt as if he had just climbed Mt. Everest.

Ken took a deep breath. From this height, Helen was even smaller than from the lower branch. He couldn't hear what she was saying. But miraculously his fear had dissipated. He sensed that he was on the verge of a quantum leap in achievement.

After another deep breath, with quiet deliberation, he launched himself from the safety of the perch. In a flash, the demons of his worst fears possessed him again. His whole body tensed the moment he was airborne. He was soon plummeting vertically down in a tailspin, like the first time, frozen stiff in panic. The air rushed past him upwards, rustling his feathers and lifting his comb and mane skywards. He was the very icon of fear. His wings hung like heavy sacks of lead by his sides.

'At this height, I'm going to be smashed to a

pulp on the ground below if I don't pull out of this nosedive this very instant,' he told himself.

Over the whistling of the rushing air, he could not hear Helen screaming, "Flap your wings! Flap your wings!"

But that's what he involuntarily did. He flapped his wings in panic and screamed in high-pitched terror.

Suddenly he was no longer falling. He had pulled out of the stall. He was airborne now, buoyant on his on power. Ken knew right away that he was no longer powerless. He was in control. There were things he could do. He began flapping his wings in a controlled, measured manner. His trajectory steadied. The feeling was exhilarating. He rode the oncoming breeze, climbing several feet higher before aiming for the grassy knoll by the banks of the pond. As he powered himself toward terra firma, he even allowed himself the luxury of a flourish, banking first to the right, then left, and then right again in an 'S' before his feet made contact with the dead grass. He landed running, letting out a whoop of joy.

Helen breathed a huge sigh of relief. She was by his side in a jiffy.

"Congratulations! You flew! You actually flew!"

For once, Ken was at a loss for words. He merely grinned.

Helen smiled elfishly as she added, "But you could have awakened the dead with your initial screams."

"I guess I must have sounded like Ma when the coyotes came," replied Ken smiling sheepishly.

Ken was overjoyed that he had come through victorious.

But there was not going to be any respite.

"You are going back up once more for another try," Helen said firmly.

"*What?*" Ken was flabbergasted.

"Yes, you heard me. The best way to vanquish the enemy is to finish him off once and for all and not give him a chance to regroup his forces."

"Can't we do it tomorrow?" Ken protested. But he knew better. Helen had a point.

The next attempt was a substantial improvement. He did not stall. From the take-off, he flew with purpose and control. Only the landing was a little gawky, stumbling as his feet hit a clump of grass.

"Not bad! Not bad at all" applauded Helen. "I knew you had it in you the first time I saw you.

Quite the high-flier now, eh?"

It was Ken's turn to surprise Helen.

"I'm going to go back up and do it one more time. I botched the landing. It wasn't perfect. Must strike while the iron is hot."

Ken kept his word.

Just before he touched the ground, he appeared to hover momentarily over the spot for a fraction of a second before alighting gently, for a flawless landing—a perfect two-pointer, without the slightest stumble—the envy of any world-class gymnast.

"Show-off!" teased Helen.

Ken grinned. He walked ten feet tall.

"I cannot believe I did it! I would never have even dreamed of flying if it were not for you, Helen," he said gratefully.

"You did it yourself," was all Helen said with a smile.

But the sense of achievement was as much Helen's as it was Ken's.

Ken positively glowed. "I feel like the Red Baron!" But he added quickly, "Though, as a pacifist, I wouldn't want to hurt anyone, let alone shoot down airplanes. Can't wait to tell Ma. She'll be proud, I think."

"She will be. But don't let it go to your head. See you tomorrow!" With that Helen turned and glided towards the pond.

Ma was all smiles when Ken reached her in the meadow.

"Well done, Ken!" she said proudly.

"Ma, you already know?"

Ken was mildly disappointed that he could not surprise Ma with his accomplishment.

"I was watching your antics from here. Remember the higher you fly, the more visible you are to others. Congratulations my son! You have no idea how happy I am."

"Ma, will you fly with me?"

"I wish I could, Ken. But my aim is to be the best laying hen there ever was. And that goal requires that I be a plump waddler, rather than a slim high-flier. You go right ahead. Keep improving your flying skills. Just don't get into trouble at the farm. Get back in before the evening curfew."

+++

"Helen, I have a purpose in life now—to master the art of flying," announced Ken the next day.

"That's not a bad aim at all to have. But flying

is not everything. You will learn all you need to in double quick time. There is much more to master in life than flight," responded Helen.

"Sadly, for us chickens and, I guess for most humans, the sole purpose of life is the avoidance death," Ken admitted gloomily.

"But, ironically, death can never be avoided. It can only be deferred or postponed for a time. It's a dead cert. Pardon the pun. Yet, many deceive themselves into thinking that they have cheated death for good. Buying time is not a permanent victory. They are only fooling themselves."

"What then is the purpose of life?" asked Ken.

"What! You too!" exclaimed Helen rolling her eyes.

"Why? Is that not a fair question?" Ken would not easily give up.

"My first thought is: Who are we to ask? And why do we need to ask? We have been created and have been gifted life. Our mandate is to live. Just live. Plain and simple. Why must we question why we were given the gift of life?"

Ken stared uncomprehendingly.

Helen continued. "Man keeps searching for rationale and purpose. They need a purpose to drive their lives."

"What about us? Is there a meaning to our lives?" persisted Ken.

"Philosophy is an absolute waste of time, if you ask me. For Man, it is all about them. They still behave as if they were the center of the universe. They think everything else revolves around them—the whole galaxy, the entire universe! It's actually the other way around. Yet, they lord it over the rest of creation."

"But that does not answer my question."

"Leave existential anxieties to Man. They have nothing better to do. You and me, we are pieces of a gigantic and ever-changing mosaic, full of color and vitality. This montage of life is incomplete without us, however brief our time or insignificant our roles on this earth might be."

"It is not easy not to think ..." Ken demurred.

"Live life to the fullest! And by that I don't mean in debauchery and depravity. A life lived in simplicity, and love, and with respect for others is the sacred purpose. That is what we Canada geese live by. Think enough to assess risks. Leave excess thinking to Man. They think and think. And then they think some more. They overthink everything and make their brief lives seem miserably long— and yet not long enough."

+++

Ken practiced his flying every day. Instead of walking, he flew even short distances within the farm. Inside the shack, before turning in for the night, he reveled in hovering above the others like one of those police helicopters. Only Ma's rebuke, "Get down now! Right now!" brought him back to the sawdust-strewn floor.

Outdoors during the day, Ken tasted the joys of flying. Initially, he flew short distances along the sides of the pond while Helen watched from the ground.

Then they began to fly in tandem. First around the pond and then across it. Their circles widened as Ken's wings strengthened.

Helen's tribe watched his progress too. Hoover the veteran dubbed him the Flying Chicken.

"I have a question, Helen. Why do you fly in a V? Why not a W or a U or a T?" asked Ken.

"The V is the most aerodynamically efficient way to fly as a group. Man has given it a fancy name. They call the V formation a chevron. The beauty of the chevron is that it gets progressively easier towards the back. The greatest effort is needed at the front. The ones to the rear benefit from the ripples created by the ones ahead. This way we take care of the weaker ones in the group. We take turns and rotate the positions in the chevron to share the toil and the strain."

"Wow! You don't swarm around haphazardly here and there like other birds. Your tribe is very organized and methodical."

"It pays to be systematic and methodical. And we have to be—to be able to fly long distances with team members of varying abilities. A cross-country flight is a meticulously orchestrated and intricately choreographed song and dance of life. It is truly a sacred journey—full of awe and devotion."

+++

One day, Judy and Daniel, two of the first timers, joined them. The four of them circled the pond three times nonstop before alighting on the grassy knoll.

"This chicken can fly like us!" Judy said as she laughed uninhibitedly.

Then they took off again, away from the pond this time, for half a mile, before veering to the left to swing back again to Helen's group.

"The joys of flying are infectious. And so are the joys of achievement and working together,"

Helen said.

"I don't know which gives me greater joy—the sheer charm of flying or mastering this new skill."

"There is more to come. Much more. Knowledge and wisdom are ever-widening circles of delight," Helen said with quiet assurance.

"I can't wait to learn more!"

"There will be times when you might regret having said that. The path of learning is not as easy as sashaying down a ramp," Helen said with a smile.

"I will try my very best to be a model student," said Ken earnestly. Helen could not help smiling.

"To those who fly, are the hidden secrets of the world revealed," Helen said mysteriously.

"How so?" queried Ken.

"Up there, there is freedom. Unimaginable freedom. There are no obstacles. No fences, no barricades, no barriers, no walls. No national boundaries. It is one continuous open space."

"I never thought of the heavens that way. Here's something else I have always wondered about. You fly so high in the sky, you may know the answer. Every day I lift my eyes to the heavens and see the fluffy white clouds that float against the blue backdrop. Where does the world end? Are we in a glass box like the one in which Ryan keeps his pet ants?"

"The world does not end. I don't know how to explain this. The earth is a solid ball within a ball of air," Helen explained.

"That's difficult to understand, Helen. Ryan's basketball has air *inside*—not on the outside."

"The Creator made it all. We do not need to understand everything to be able to enjoy what we are blessed with. But seriously, up there, there is unity. There are no schisms or divisions such as there are here on the ground. No states, no countries. No borders, no boundaries. Just one unbroken sky girding the earth, blanketing all the dissensions below."

"You're waxing poetic now!" exclaimed Ken.

"It is actually true. Up there, there are no burning deserts, no humid forests, no seas, no rushing waters, no farms, no concrete jungles. No hills, no valleys."

"What about storms, tornadoes, cyclones, hurricanes?" Ken asked.

"Life is not all plain sailing. We need to take the rough with the smooth. Sure, there are frightening storms sometimes. We either fly around them or bide our time till the storm is past. We do not compete against nature."

"Flying sounds almost invincible to me!"

"On the contrary. We are very vulnerable when up there. Our underbellies are open to the lead bullets of gun lovers and hunters. They stand knee-deep in mud, camouflaged in grass, making faux duck calls to shoot us out of the sky. They have no sense of fairness. If only it were a level playing field."

"The hunter would not stand a chance against you if it was an even fight," asserted Ken.

"I am a pacifist. I do not want to kill anyone. If it was a fair contest not unto death … of brains …"

"You are a genius!" gushed Ken in awe.

"Nah! I'm just an ornery goose. To quote the famous detective, 'I'm neither a dunce nor a thaumaturge.'"

"Detective? Which one? Sherlock Holmes? Hercule Poirot? Inspector Maigret?"

"No, Wolfe. Rex Stout's Nero Wolfe."

## 6  I Believe; So, I Fly

A second winter storm arrived, confining Ken again indoors in the shack with everyone else for the next eight days. Ken's despondency this time was worse than the first time. Only the presence of Ma saved him from being bullied and tormented. Ken did not enjoy one bit the proximity of these 'coarse, earthy louts', as he labeled them in his head.

But Ken took advantage of the bedlam around him to tell Ma of his extended flights with the visitors.

"I knew that already," she said simply.

"How did you know?"

"You know better than to ask that by now." She paused before continuing. "I knew from the time you were born that you were capable of extraordinary accomplishments."

+++

The day they were let out, Ken rushed to the fence to look for Helen. Like after the first storm, Helen looked as gorgeous as Ken looked scruffy, giving the distinct impression that she thrived in snow storms. Ken joyfully flew over the barrier to the freedom of the open space.

After they had caught up, Ken remembered Larry standing forlorn on his visit and brought up the subject of Larry's aloofness. "You didn't tell me the whole story about that Larry guy. Why's he the way he is?" asked Ken.

Helen hesitated a moment before she shared Larry's story.

"It's not an easy story to tell. He was not that way till his wife died. Larry was a happy-go-lucky guy. Gregarious, always. An affectionate and devoted husband. And a good friend. He smiled all the time. Then Beth, his wife, died and he changed. Since her death, he wants to be left alone. Nobody knows him now. I sometimes think he does not know even himself anymore," said Helen sadly.

"Why did he take his wife's death so much to heart? We have deaths happening all the time in our clan on the farm. Death's a weekly affair. We get over it. We move on."

"Relationships in your culture are different from ours. We mate for life. We are monogamous."

"What does that mean?" Ken was puzzled.

"It means we are loyal to our spouses. We are not adulterous. We pair, male and female, and we pair for life. We do not hook up on the spur of the moment."

"No one-night stands for us Canada geese," she added pointedly.

"Really? That's not how we Rhode Island Reds live life. But how did she die?"

"It happened on our pilgrimage here last year—my first long-distance journey—near the Finger Lakes of New York State. We had crossed over from the home province of Ontario in Canada into the United States. Everything was going swimmingly well. The weather was perfect for flying and we were making good progress towards the first staging post in Amish territory in Pennsylvania for some well-earned rest. For some reason, due to clear air turbulence, if I remember right, we had descended from our cruising altitude. It was a beautiful, late fall day. The sky and the lake were both a deep azure, I still recall. Suddenly, out of the blue, without any warning at all ... Bang! Bang! Bang! ... shots rang out. The next thing we knew, Beth who was flying next to me, was plummeting to the ground like a stone. Me and Larry, who was on the other side of Beth, instinctively dropped out of the formation. When he saw her twisted body lying lifeless on the ground he bawled like a child. After circling the motionless Beth several times, we descended to her side. But when we saw the hunter and his son coming to get Beth, we scrambled back into the air in the nick of time. The hunter raised his gun to his shoulder and started shooting at us."

Helen paused, overcome by the thoughts of that day.

"They stopped shooting when they reached Beth. The hunter bent down and picked up Beth's bloodstained body by her neck and stuffed it into a canvas bag held by the son. The father had a big grin on his face. The joy of stupid hunters. When the son saw Beth's body close at hand, his face turned ashen. I would like to believe that, at that very moment, the joy hunting was forever lost for him. As for us, there was nothing more to be done."

Helen paused again momentarily.

"We flew out of range of their shotguns and rejoined the rest of our team that had made an unscheduled landing by the lake. This was an emergency. Larry, disconsolate, wailed for his dead love. We tried to console him, but to no avail. He would not be comforted. He took off again and I followed him. Larry circled above the hunter and his son carrying Beth's body. The hunter laughed diabolically as he fired in our direction. He even had his son take potshots at us. I moved out of range of the guns. Larry didn't care. He circled right above Beth's body. He was lucky not to get shot himself. I think he'd have preferred to have been shot—to have died with his beloved. I pleaded with Larry to return to the team. He did so reluctantly. We did not fly further that day. We camped right by the Finger Lakes. We all tried our very best, but Larry was inconsolable."

"And he has remained the same ever since?"

"Yes. Larry is a broken being. A shadow of his former self. He never reverted to his former jovial self. He was forever altered," said Helen.

"Isn't remarrying allowed in your tribe? Why didn't he marry again? Didn't you try to help him?" asked Ken with a knowing look.

"Yes, remarriage is permitted and even encouraged in our tribe for widowers. But, no, Larry did not remarry. He told me one day he could not love again. He had lost the capacity to love. His overwhelming grief never left him. I don't think he ever got over the abrupt shock of her passing. Life did not make any sense to him, he told me once. I was the only female he confided in after Beth's passing. She and I were best friends. I grieved for her too. I still do. A beautiful life unjustly snuffed in the prime of life. But I could not have accepted Larry as spouse for Beth's sake. I told him we could be friends. He was fine with that. That's what we are. Just friends. Nothing more. But in a way, it is more than anything else."

Ken was silent for a while.

Then he said softly, "I am too moved by Beth's story to say anything. But I wonder about death. Is there a heaven for us?"

"The Creator shall save both man and beast," intoned Helen solemnly.

"You really believe that?" Ken was skeptical.

"I didn't make this up, Ken. It is in the Book."

"Why do you think that hunter killed Beth? Why was he teaching his son to kill?"

"As the Bard wrote, they kill us for their sport," Helen said wearily. "And to satisfy their bottomless appetites."

There was a long silence after that.

Then Ken cleared his throat, and lowering his voice to bass, sang 'Swing Low, Sweet Chariot,'

Johnny Cash style.

When Ken was done, Helen raised her eyes to the heavens and sang with feeling, '*This World Is Not My Home.*'

"Songs like these bring tears to my eyes every time I hear them," said Helen.

"You know, Helen, if what you told earlier about heaven is true, what would be the most wonderful part?" Ken asked with a beatific smile.

"No. What?"

"Man would not kill us anymore—neither for sport nor for gluttony. Since, by its very definition, there are no deaths in heaven, there cannot be any killing there either."

"Well done! You are learning. You are well on your way to becoming an autodidact," said Helen smiling.

Seeing the puzzled look on Ken's face, she clarified.

"A self-taught person. Self-learning is truly the only way to learn anything."

"Thanks. I may have unconsciously connected to the Cosmos, the collective consciousness of the Universe!"

"Which is always good. Afflatus, it is called."

Then sobering up, she added. "I feel sorry for your tribe. Unfortunately for you all, you are Man's most desired meat. They even think your soup is good for their souls. They don't have a clue! The soul doesn't reside in the belly, where they think it does!"

"Ha, ha. But it hurts when I laugh."

"You are only slightly better off than the hapless turkeys who are slaughtered en masse every year."

"Yes, Ma told us about the turkeys. She said they are a doomed tribe."

"What a terrible fate! To be decimated every year! For Man, it is thanksgiving, family time, and rejoicing. For the luckless turkeys, it is annual genocide, mourning, and lamentation," Helen said dolefully.

"How I wish they would take a leaf out of the book of the Malayalis of the Indian state of Kerala. They forego all meat and fish for their annual festival of Onam. Irrespective of their religion, they all turn vegetarian for the duration of the festival. Their sumptuous feasts are completely meatless. Now, how wonderful is that! The whole creation, all living beings, including Man, join in joyous celebration. Not Man alone at the cost of other creatures," Ken narrated beatifically.

"That would be too much to ask of Occidentals. Can you imagine the hue and cry that would cause here? But what I can't understand is this. Why must they *all* stuff themselves with *only* turkey on Thanksgiving? Can't they at least even it out a bit with beef, pork, and fish and so on? Why must the turkeys alone bear the brunt of man's perverted sense of gratitude? Do they even consider the impact the annual ritual genocide has on the poor turkeys?" Helen lamented.

"Ma told us that the President pardons two turkeys every year."

Helen was livid. "Big deal! What a farce! He pardons *two* turkeys while tens of *millions* are slaughtered? What a cruel joke! Is it any wonder he has not acknowledged the Armenian genocide committed by the Ottoman Turks!"

"Very true. Thanks for leaving chicken out in the alternate meat suggestions for Thanksgiving. But our fate is not much better. It's like living on death row from day one. But your tribe, Helen, is different. Man should love you for what you are. You don't harm anyone. You are pacifists. You don't overstay your welcome. Your tribe and the seasons are inseparable. But Ma said there are still many who hate you. But why?" asked Ken.

"Man is the planet's most mixed-up creature, eh? Once upon a time, the newcomers to the continent from Europe—themselves refugees—almost exterminated us. They hunted us to near extinction. Then they passed laws to protect us. Now that we are thriving, they want to cull us again. Man cannot stand another's prosperity—even of their own kind. If it is any consolation, they kill each other just as much as they kill us."

"I thought they killed only us birds and animals!" Ken was incredulous.

"No, they kill each other like crazy. They dropped atom bombs that killed hundreds of thousands and maimed millions over decades. The big wars almost finished Man. But they still haven't learned their lesson. Wars go on even today. For them, wars are a way to make money. Scratch the rich countries and you will find an unscrupulous arms dealer under the disguise of a benevolent do-gooder. They gouge wealth out of the misery of others."

"Ma told us about the terrible terrorists," Ken interjected.

"Now, they are a different breed altogether. And the stupidest of the lot. They even blow themselves up in order to kill others!"

"Really? That's the most insane thing I've ever

heard! Isn't it worse than cutting off the nose to spite one's face? It is literally cutting off one's own neck!" exclaimed Ken.

"It does not make any sense at all. But believe you me, it is true. They do it. All the time."

"I believe you. But what is the reason for their murderous hate for each other?" pressed Ken.

"Broadly speaking, there are two things they cannot tolerate in other people, especially those different from themselves. Religion and politics. If your religion is different, you are an infidel and must be killed. And if your politics is not modeled after Western democracy, woe betide your country! On brazenly trumped up charges, or clandestinely, they will wreck your nation and rip the fabric of your society forever."

"But isn't democracy a good thing?" Ken wanted to know.

"Sure, it is. But it is not one-size-fits-all. There are variations of it. Look at us. We have a robust democracy, and we also have equality and gender balance. But we don't go around thrusting them down other people's throats. It works for us. And that is good enough. If other tribes prefer a dictator or royalty or a clique of corrupt oligarchs, who are we to poke our bills in their affairs?

"I cannot agree more," concurred Ken.

"Meddling with others is worse than stirring up a hornet's nest. It will come back to bite you—big time. You think you destroyed them—but you pay the price later, and generally, far greater."

"You don't make democracy sound very nice."

"Man, poor thing, doesn't have much of a choice. The other camp is hardly any better. The reward for dissent is gulag, exile, or summary execution. Kulaks and ethnic minorities were wrenched from their familiar homelands unannounced and transported like herds of cattle to alien and inhospitable terrains thousands of miles away."

"Terrible. Wish we could all just live and let live," mused Ken.

"Yes. Now wouldn't that be a good thing! Look at what Man did to us. They first imprisoned us. Force-fed us their dreadful food. Clipped our wings so we couldn't fly, and, in so doing, ripped from our souls our hallowed tradition of migration. They did the exact same thing to Native Americans and the First Nations—stripped their souls bare and crushed their spirit. There is one other thing that drives their killing. Covetousness. Sheer greed. They covet the natural resources that belong to other nations."

"How terrible!" Ken was appalled.

"I agree. But again, less gruesome than Man's honor killings where people murder their own family. Their own flesh and blood! Can you believe it! Where is the honor in killing your own daughter, I ask?"

"And to think I considered Man the master of the universe," Ken shook his head in disbelief.

"Master, my foot! They are myopic lunatics! Even as we speak, they are stockpiling atomic weapons that can exterminate every single living thing on this planet in a matter of minutes—blow the whole world to smithereens and to kingdom come!"

"Wouldn't the wise thing be to voluntarily turn weapons to ploughshares?" asked Ken hesitantly.

"That is what it looks like to you and me. But not to wise Man. They keep piling them up. I ask you, just think, why would peace weapons, eh?"

They were silent for a while.

Then Helen said, "You know, what is killing Man more than war?" asked Helen.

"Disease?" ventured Ken.

"In a manner of speaking, yes. The disease of political correctness."

"*What?*" blurted out Ken. "Being nice is harmful?"

"You know, things have come to such a sorry pass that Man wants to be seen as being politically correct, even at the cost of being morally and ethically wrong," said Helen.

"You mean it's like the emperor's new clothes all over again?" Ken asked sarcastically.

"Yes, that's what it is. Political correctness is emperor's new clothes on steroids! Modern Man confuses political correctness with politeness. Just because the two words look halfway similar, does not mean they are the same thing," Helen said firmly.

"Maybe political correctness is kindness?" asked Ken.

"Kindness is not political correctness either. Being deeply unkind to oneself while being politically correct to others is not kindness. It is pathetic to see people bend over backwards to affirm what goes against the very grain of their most cherished values."

"What is the way out then?" Ken wanted to know.

"There is a way out of the quagmire. Neither approve nor condemn. Neither fawn nor hate. Let the other be. Accept them as they are. It is difficult to be impolite if you keep your mouth shut," said Helen with a smile.

"Ha, ha, not true! One can scowl and make faces and roll one's eyes, all without saying a word and be just as offensive," Ken countered.

"Point taken. But what I meant was, we do not have to react to everything. We do not need to go around as if we had Asperger's and rile everybody up. At the same time, why would we belittle our own beliefs and extol the praises of alien customs and practices of others for the sake of pleasing them and being seen as nice, even when we know full well in our hearts that they are contrary to the values we hold most dear?"

"What then? Hate them?"

"No! Not endorsing the traditions of others does not mean hating them. Everyone has the freedom and the free will to do what they want without harming others. We must respect that. We don't need to affirm values that don't match ours. But that does not mean we hate them. It's hard for a rambler and a wanderer who has seen the world to be a bigot. You cannot travel the world and hate others at the same time. And hate can never be part of anyone's value set."

"Why is that?" asked Ken.

"Because hate is not a value—love is. Hate is an unvalue!"

"You are coining new words!"

"But it is really true. It is silly to base one's likes and dislikes on feathers and pelts, which molt. That's just skin or feather deep. It is only the core that endures and that is all that matters."

"I cannot disagree with that without coming across as a xenophobe. But what does one do?" persisted Ken.

"You celebrate the core being of others and ignore the external. It is when they are rude, boorish, and violent that one needs to walk away. Otherwise there is plenty of common ground to go around. Successful travelers are all code-switchers."

"What's a code-switcher?" Ken asked.

"It's simpler than it sounds. What it means is to mold your behavior to match that of the person you are with. For me it is more than mere speaking. It has to do with the heart of your being. You cannot change your outward appearance, but you can mold your inner self to be as close as possible to the people you are with. Anyone can travel once to another culture. Only code-switchers get welcomed with open arms again and again and again."

"I can never be a code-switcher," Ken said downcast.

"Anyone can be one. It's all about being nonjudgmental. Don't be a self-righteous nosey parker is all I am saying. It's no skin off your nose what others do or how they do it! You don't have to espouse their cause or, worse, champion it. Neither insult nor applaud. Neither a bigot nor a doormat be."

"Keeping one's gob shut then is the best means of political correctness?" said Ken smiling quizzically.

"No fish ever got into trouble by keeping its mouth shut, as the Korean saying goes!"

Helen's deadpan riposte had Ken in stitches. When he got his breath back, he persisted.

"But why does Man hate your tribe so much even if you do not meddle in their affairs?"

"It is the silliest reason ever! It's all because of calls of nature."

"Calls of nature? Loud honking, you mean?"

"No. Toilets. We don't build toilets. Wherever we go, we fertilize the earth. That was the plan of the Creator. It is not only organic but also completely biodegradable, which cannot be said of Man's plastics even after a hundred years. Yet they label us as polluters! Can you believe that, eh?" Helen bristled with righteous indignation.

"If it's any comfort, we do the same as you."

"Of course, you do. We are birds. Man accuses us of dirtying their places up. But look at them! Their toilets may be spic and span, but they have made the whole earth one gigantic dung heap. Lands and oceans have become cesspools of their deadly plastic and toxic wastes which never decompose. We see from the air, when we fly, the colossal destruction of the environment by Man ... the enormous landfills they create to get rid of their garbage ... and the huge square miles of swirling islands of plastic waste in the ocean. Unsuspecting creatures on land and sea who mistake Man's litter for food, pay the ultimate price."

"It's obvious, you care deeply about the environment. But why? We are here for too short a time, aren't we?"

"That's the fallacy of Man's thinking. They think of the environment as something external forgetting that they are also part and parcel of the ecology and the environment."

Helen fell silent before adding soberly, "We care for the environment because we not only did not create it, we also do not own it. We are sojourners. Renters, wherever we go. We are itinerant serfs and emancipated muzhiks. It is not for us to degrade the environment that is part of us and of which we are an inseparable part."

"Well said. But are they really trying to kill you?" Ken asked.

"Here's a funny story for you. Welland, the town close to ours, had a town hall meeting to discuss ways of controlling our population. They discussed various options. Addling our eggs, setting the dogs on us (those vicious Border Collies, no less), of upping the hunting quota, and even having a goose shooting contest."

"They certainly have their knives out for you!"

"Of course. We have no white privilege. But back to the story. An unkempt, old geezer stood up to suggest that the most humane way to check our burgeoning numbers was not to kill us in cold blood but to steal our eggs and, instead of addling them, make free omelets for the homeless. 'We'll be killing two birds with one stone,' he had added facetiously."

"Why is it funny?" Ken asked.

"That was the only sensible and humane suggestion compared to using guns and dogs, or drones and algorithms to decimate us. But that man was shouted down. There was no money in his idea for the big corporations."

"How can Man be so cruel?"

"Mankind kills other creatures with impunity. As flies to wanton boys ..."

"What's that?" Ken asked puzzled.

"They kill us for their sport," completed Helen wearily.

"Oh!" said Ken in awe.

"But if it's any consolation, they kill their own offspring too," Helen said gravely.

"No way! Get out of here!" exclaimed Ken.

"No, I'm not making this up. They actually do. They kill their offspring while still in the mother's womb."

"You mean they have devised ways to restrict the populations of the groups they hate?"

"They wish! But no. It is the mothers themselves who voluntarily have their unborn children killed. It is the most ghoulish thing imaginable!"

Ken had no words. All color drained from his

comb which drooped like a wet flower after a deluge.

Helen continued. "This is the unvarnished truth. Women fiercely assert their right to kill their own defenseless offspring. They call it reproductive rights. But, in reality, it is killing rights. Reproductive rights would be the right to bear children—not kill them in cold blood. And then they have the temerity to parade in the streets posturing themselves as progressive, caring, pacifists who bleed for the violence in distant, strife-torn regions of the world."

Ken was ashen-faced and speechless.

Helen continued with her diatribe against feticide.

"How can murdering your own defenseless offspring be feminism? Where is the maternal instinct? They are killing their own femininity even as they kill their own babies." She paused. "I tell you, there is barely squeezing room between conservative fanatics on the one side and permissive liberals on the other."

"Terrible!" was all Ken could say.

"You know what's worse? In some patriarchal societies, they selectively kill female fetuses so they can have more sons than daughters. Oh, the devilish misuse of scientific advancement! Where is gender equity and fairness!"

"I am sickened to my stomach. I have heard enough," Ken said wearily.

"It is not pretty, I know. Humans are mostly inhuman. It is downright depressing. Come, let's shake off the blues by going for a spin, eh? Let 's check to see if Judy and Daniel would care to join us."

In answer to Helen's honk, Judy and Daniel flew up, but along with them also came Nancy and Bruce. To their astonishment, Larry took off too and trailed a little behind them for a while. When they climbed higher over the Baltimore-Washington Parkway and the Beltway to avoid the hot fumes of the traffic, Larry speeded up to complete the chevron's leading right edge, next to Ken. They flew parallel to Route 193 all the way to Lake Artemesia in College Park. When the other five descended to the water, Larry wordlessly flew beside Ken around the northern end of the lake several times before Larry also glided down to the water. Ken continued his flight training alone. He made steep climbs without stalling and equally steep dives from which he pulled out at a safe height. He felt that his muscles had greater power now than they had when he had started out on this adventure of flight. To test his powers further, he raised his speed in short bursts to the limits of his endurance. At higher speeds, he increased the bank as he made sweeping turns. Ken exulted as the earth tilted below in sync with him on these curving loops.

It was a tired Ken who flew back with Helen and her five team mates.

Ryan had skipped gym to do the day's homework. He looked momentarily up from the complicated calculus question to stare out of the window. What he saw made him rub his eyes in disbelief. He wondered if he was dreaming. If his eyes were not deceiving him, there was Ken, gliding into the backyard like a bird. The differentiation function he was trying to solve was forgotten in an instant. He ran out to see for himself.

Ken, by the water-trough, pretended not to notice Ryan running towards him barefoot and all excited. Even before Ryan opened his mouth, Ken knew the jig was up.

"Hey, you, rascal! Since when have you taken to flying around the farm?"

Ken's initial reaction was to feign innocence but if he could not trust Ryan, who else could he? He fluttered his wings to rise gently and hover like a helicopter at Ryan's chest level demonstrating his prowess. Ryan reached out to hold him.

"I knew from the beginning you're special! Don't worry, your secret is safe with me!"

Ken perched on Ryan's shoulder and sang '*You Raise Me Up*' fervently.

When Ken ended the song, Ryan held him up with both hands and released him upwards into the air. Ken joyously flew higher and performed a circle before gently alighting again on Ryan's shoulder.

## 7  OLD DOG, NEW TRICKS

Ken and Helen began spending more time together. Now it was always Ken who came over to Helen's side of the fence. They drew much delight in doing things together, however insignificant or run-of-the-mill. Flying around, foraging for food, or just walking about in the vicinity of the pond.

One such day, after some strenuous flying exercises, they were standing around preening themselves on the grassy verge close to the edge of the pond.

The attack took them totally unawares.

One moment they were languidly basking in the warmth of the afternoon sun. The next, all hell had broken loose. Out of the corner of his left eye Ken saw a gigantic brown blur lunging towards him. And simultaneously he heard a deep, bloodcurdling growl. It all happened in a flash. Ken felt a sharp tug on his left wing. Startled, he wrenched his arm free and hurled himself instinctively upward into the air, cackling angrily. Almost in unison Helen took to the air, honking loudly, evading the attacker who had now sprung in her direction. Helen's cohorts by the pond's edge, hearing her danger calls, picked up the refrain. Honking stridently, they flew up in a frenzy from the water's edge, noisily flapping their wings. The other gaggles in the vicinity joined in the chorus. It was sheer bedlam.

Ken flew up to the safety of the nearest tree. Helen alighted next to him, balancing herself precariously on the branch on her flat feet.

"Are you OK?" she asked anxiously.

Ken was clearly in shock. He shook his head.

Looking down they saw a large German shepherd staring up at them, barking viciously. That had been the brown blur. On the ground behind the hound lay scattered four of Ken's shiny red and gold wing feathers. Further away stood the dog's master holding the rolled-up leash, squinting upward to look at them through thick glasses.

Helen's teammates circled above the tree they were on till Helen confirmed they were safe.

Ken examined his left wing again. There was blood from where the feathers had been yanked out cruelly by the hound.

Helen read the hurt in Ken's eyes.

"Whew! That was a close call!" she said trying to calm him.

"You can say that again!" grimaced a still panting Ken, his heart still thudding in his heart like the hooves of a galloping horse. "The scoundrel! He snuck upon me. He didn't give me a fair chance."

"That's the evil one's hallmark. His game plan is to catch us napping. Unprepared. We need to keep our eyes peeled all the time. Can't afford to let our guard down even for an instant."

Ken turned to Helen with an ominous look. "The mutt drew blood. I won't let him get away with this. Let's give it back to them both, Helen. You go for the human. I'll take the dog who bit me."

He paused before adding famously, "I'm no chicken."

Helen smiled briefly. She did not need a second prompt.

She made a kamikaze dive straight for the man's head, honking in anger. The man threw up his arms as if in surrender. The dog barked and leapt in the air, but Helen was beyond his reach. After two feigned attacks, Helen swerved and swooped down suddenly. She whacked the man on the side of his head with her right wing knocking his baseball cap to the ground. As the dog leaped again to his master's defense, Ken hurtled from behind straight for the back of the unsuspecting mutt's head. In one fell swoop he planted a nasty peck on the top of the canine's head and dragged his right claw vengefully along the side of yelping dog's head on the upswing, out of reach, to land on a branch of the tree opposite. Ken had evened the score, drawing blood. The man and his dog, scared out of their wits, turned tail.

Helen screamed after the fleeing pair, "Keep your cur leashed, you moron!"

Ken followed her to the ground. "Now that was *pretty satisfying*, wasn't it? Straight out of Hitchcock!"

"You were quite the Red Baron, eh!" Helen said in admiration.

They both laughed merrily in the joy of victory.

Nevertheless, they both knew how close they had been to death.

"I am not going to take anything for granted

anymore," Ken said gravely.

"The group next to ours lost a pair to a Massasauga rattlesnake in the grasslands of Bruce Peninsula last year. The female was bit first and the male who wouldn't leave got bit also and made the ultimate sacrifice. Snakes are the evilest of all creatures there is."

"Yes, Ma warned us all about snakes. She said they sneak up on you noiselessly and you are gone in an instant," said Ken.

"I myself I learned a lesson many months ago at the pier at Port Dalhousie. A dog very nearly bit my head off. How I hate those pampered pets! Do not suspect everyone you meet but do not trust everyone either. That's the key to a long life," Helen responded.

"I look at cats and dogs and think ..." began Ken.

"Don't get me started!" interrupted Helen. "A pet is the surrogate spouse of modern Man. You know why Man loves them so much? Pets are servile and cannot argue back—at least not in human language. And they are completely dependent on the mercy of the owner. This makes the owner feel important and wanted. Pathetic! The slave owner mentality of Man is still alive and well!"

"I don't know much about pets," said Ken.

"The owners think of themselves as the lords of their pets. But it is the owner who follows them with a plastic bag picking up their feces. Tell me now, who is the servant—the animal or its night soil collector? It is the most ridiculous thing!"

"They treat pets as if they were their babies?" asked Ken.

"Loving pets up to a certain extent, is fine. But in the West, they carry it too far. A pet is treated like a child or grandchild. And the best part is that the pet will always remain a child and will never grow into a rebellious teenager like Dennis who will one day call their bluff."

"I never thought of pets that way!" Ken exclaimed.

"It gets worse. Pets are over pampered. There are shelters for strays while homeless humans are out on their ears braving the elements just like us."

"You are jealous! You want to be a pet!" teased Ken.

"No way! I'd rather die. Give me the freedom of the skies and of the outdoors where I can be all that the Creator made me to be. To live a cocooned life, even in comfort, as a slave to selfish morons is a fate worse than hell."

Ken did not need another prompt. He sang *'Home! Home On The Range!'* with soulful intensity.

That day Ryan found the last piece of the puzzle. Unseen from a far corner of the farm, he watched Ken fly high in the sky and cavort above the tree tops with six Canada geese. Excepting for the fact that Ken did not outwardly look like the others, there was little to choose between him and the Canada geese in aerial prowess and maneuvers.

+++

The days flew by. Gradually, imperceptibly, the days elongated in the rising warmth of the sun. Though it was still cold, it looked as if the chance of any more snowfalls appeared remote. The only snow that remained on the ground was what lay hidden from the sun in the shadows of the grove. Winter was clearly relenting.

Now that the water was not as cold, Helen decided it was time to break the news to Ken.

"There is one other thing you need to learn as a member of the bird family—and especially as an adopted member of our tribe," said Helen.

"I thought flying was the only hurdle. And a very difficult one at that. I'm just about getting the hang of it. What now? What is next? Walk on burning coal? Tap dance over a barbecue?"

"Now don't be sarcastic! It is something even simpler than flying. Matter of fact, you don't actually have to do anything. Now, how do you like that, eh?"

Ken looked at her skeptically. "Is there some kind of secret initiation ceremony like that of the Freemasons or worse that involves drinking blood or mutilation or some other awful act."

"No! We are not that kind! How could you even think that?" Helen acted more outraged than she actually was.

"Then tell me. What is it that I have to do?"

"I'll tell you. It is something we do every day. Swim."

"*Swim?*" Ken was horrified. We chicken, we aren't fish. It makes no sense at all!"

"Birds were created to fly *and* swim. Some don't and that's their prerogative. Waters are a good thing. That's from where we get some of our food. It also keeps us clean. Most of all, it is great fun. You will love it. I guarantee you, you will."

"Helen, you don't understand. You don't understand at all! My tribe is not particularly fond of water, other than for drinking when thirsty. I

116

had a near-death experience when I was three weeks old—nearly drowned in the water-trough."

"Well, you know by now, achievement can never be found in the comfort zone. It always lies outside of it. Once you thought you couldn't fly. You can now. This is also something you think you cannot do but you very easily can. If it were not, would I even suggest it?"

"You will be the death of me yet, Helen," Ken said shaking his head.

+++

Ken was not ready for swimming the next day. He stayed on his side of the boundary and spoke to Helen through the chain-link fence.

"You're stressed out about the swim, aren't you?" Helen asked gently.

"Not really ..." began Ken but quickly changed his tack. "Who am I kidding? The very thought of the water scares me. I need time to think this through. Makes my head swim, if you ask me!"

"No pressure. It was just a suggestion. I know for a certainty that you will love being in the water—once you get the knack of it. But I won't force you to swim or to attempt anything else that you are not comfortable with."

"Thanks, Helen."

"We are all given the power to make our own choices. There is no compulsion either to do this or not do that. There are many among my tribe who choose not to fly south any more in winter. They stay right there in Ontario all the year round. It is their decision. They have taken the easy way out. But they are a shadow of what they can be."

"Easy way out? What about the cold they have to endure?" Ken was puzzled.

"Granted, it is colder there than here. But in recent years—thanks to Man—it is not as cold anymore as it used to be. Mankind is heating up this planet like nobody's business. But the cold is not the issue. The slackers have let the easy life go to their heads. The majority of them have become enslaved to Man's poisonous fast food, receiving in their bodies obesity and other plagues as their just reward. Others ruin their lives and break the hearts of their spouses with promiscuity. And for security, they place their trust in Man's wildlife laws rather than relying on their own Creator-given powers."

"If those geese choose not to fly, why must I, a chicken, learn to swim?" asked Ken. "Give me one good reason."

"You don't *have* to swim. But you would not

have attained your full persona—all that you were created to be. Water completes your restoration."

Ken did not appear convinced.

"Have you already forgotten Wilma, the polio-stricken sprint queen, Ken? Push yourself just a teeny-weeny bit! If you don't, you know, you will be the mascot for underachievers, playing well below your ability. You'll be the one who does not take any chances. Calculated risks worth taking. What have you got to lose?"

That pricked the pride of the Red Baron in Ken. He agreed to give swimming a try.

"I'm not a scaredy cat!" said Ken with feigned bravado.

As Ken did not want to be embarrassed in front of Helen's team members, they flew to Greenbelt Lake in Buddy Attick Park but found it too congested with birds in the water and humans on the shore. So, they flew on to the other, Lake Artemesia in nearby College Park and landed on the shore close to the water. Immediately on landing, Helen waded straight into the pond without a moment's wait.

Ken, despite his nervousness, could not resist a wisecrack.

"Nicely done! Like a duck takes to water," Ken sniggered nervously.

Helen did not ignore the jibe.

"Come on out on the water, you chicken-livered rooster," she jeered in jest.

Ken's first essay in the water, like his first shot at flying, almost ended in tragi-comic disaster. He stepped gingerly into the water, shivering involuntarily as the cold water lapped his bright yellow feet.

Taking baby steps, he inched forward till the water was up to his ankles.

A few more steps and he was knee-deep. The water now grazed his belly.

He was surprised that the cold did not penetrate the feathers.

'There must be some truth to what Helen said. It does not feel half as cold as I had imagined,' he said to himself.

He must have stayed rooted to the spot because he heard Helen, who had turned around to watch his progress, urge him on.

"You are almost there. The longer you dilly-dally, the colder it's going to feel. Get it over with," Helen called out.

He took half a step forward, not knowing that the sandy shelf sloped steeply at that point. In an instant, he was floating, water-borne. An involuntary gasp escaped his lips. But the initial panic vanished as suddenly as it had appeared.

Ken stole a quick glance at Helen who seemed to be beckoning him farther out. He had no desire to move into deeper waters so soon. Instead, he decided to turn to the left and float parallel and close to the shore.

Then it happened. While attempting to make the turn, his nervousness caused his center of gravity to displace and he listed to the left. Ken flapped his wings frantically to correct the tilt, which only made matters worse. Kicking his legs in desperation he sought the floor but in vain. Before he knew it, he was on his side. When his head hit the water, the chilly water stung his left eye and flooded his mouth and nostrils. Ken's dread turned to full-blown panic. He thrashed his wings around in fright, sinking further. As his head went under, he gagged and screamed in sheer terror.

Helen was by his side in a flash. A sharp nudge from her and he was upright again, his feet touching the sandy bottom. He spluttered as he stumbled the last few steps back to the shore.

"For a moment, I thought you were putting on an act." Helen's attempt at levity was met with a withering look from Ken.

As he shook himself dry, Helen teased him playfully.

"No offense, but you *are* a terrible swimmer. No doubt about it. You would even drown in the Dead Sea. You are that bad."

"Didn't I tell you I have pathological fear of water? You still coerced me into making a fool of myself," Ken said accusingly.

"Oh, come on! I was only kidding! It is no disgrace to give it a shot. The losers are the ones who never try."

"Easy for you to say," grumbled Ken.

"You know, Ken, the most important victories in life are not over others. They are over our own inner fears."

"Why don't you just give up on me? What makes you persist?" asked Ken.

"We have been through this once before with your flying. Now I'll share a personal secret with you. Something only my immediate family knows. I haven't told this to anyone else. I was born a scrawny weakling—the runt of the brood. I could hardly stand, let alone waddle. Most mothers give up on their sickly children. I would have died an early death. The survival of the fittest and all that balderdash."

Helen paused. Ken waited, raptly attentive.

"But Mom never gave up on me. When the others told her it was a waste of time, she was furious. 'How dare you! She is my child! My own flesh and blood! She WILL survive. And not just survive—she will be the best.' Mom gave more time and attention to me than she did to my able-bodied siblings."

"Our mothers are very similar!" whispered Ken.

"Mom patiently taught me to walk. Even when my feeble legs would buckle under me and I would keel over in a flapping, helpless heap, she would not give up. Mom would encourage me. She would goad me. Mom made me want to try again and again and again. I never felt the shame of failure. Never ever felt being less than."

"I wouldn't have guessed by looking at you that you were not lithe and athletic all your life," said Ken.

"No, I was the feeblest gosling of the whole lot. But Mom persisted. She nudged me to the puddles of fetid seaweed on the beach. I feasted on them along with the others. And slowly, I grew. My legs strengthened. And so did my wings. I walked. In good time, I flew, albeit a little later than the others."

"Swimming must have been a lot easier?" asked Ken.

"That's the thing. You would think a goose would take to the water from the get-go. Not in my case. I was mortally scared of the water. Mom's patience again saved the day. She stepped into the water with me and stayed by my side till all my fears dissolved like snowflakes on a balmy day."

"Seeing you now who would guess that you were once hydrophobic!" Ken grinned.

"After I had slain my fears and conquered my physical disabilities, I thanked Mom one day. She would have none of it. 'That's what mothers are for,' was what she said. She then told me the story of Aren."

"Is he of your tribe?"

"No, he is Armenian. Aren's grandfather was an affluent political leader. But in a swift Stalinist purge he was executed, and all his property and wealth were confiscated by the state. The family, including son Raphael, Aren's father-to-be, who was twenty years old at the time, was banished to the gulags in Kazakhstan. On their release after two years of forced labor, Raphael returned to marry Maria, who soon gave birth to their first child, Aren. Their joy knew no bounds. But in a few months, their world came crashing down yet again when they discovered that their new-born son, Aren, did not respond to the stimuli of sound. It was apparent that Aren could not hear. The practice at that time was for parents to hand over their disabled children to the state, to live the rest of their lives in mercy homes, hidden from the public eye. But Raphael and Maria refused to give up on their precious son, Aren."

"It must have been very difficult to go against the system?" asked Ken.

"It was. But they were courageous. They petitioned for Aren to study in a regular school with other children. Maria, the mother, went to school each day with Aren and sat with him through elementary and middle schools. At home, Raphael, the father, helped Aren with homework and reading. One of the early victories was to teach Aren, who could not hear, to speak. Raphael and Maria poured themselves into bringing up and educating Aren. And their efforts paid off. Aren passed high school with flying colors. There was no stopping him after that. He went on to college where he soared way above the others, graduating with outstanding honors. To cut a long story short, Aren is now a renowned engineer in Yerevan."

"Wow! What a story!" Ken was completely bowled over.

"Yes, amazing, isn't it? Had Raphael and Maria not believed in their son, Aren would have vegetated in a home for disabled children. He may not have survived his teens. And his talents would have forever been lost."

"Every parent should be like Raphael and Maria!"

"So, will you have another go at swimming again?"

"After stories like those, how can I refuse?"

Ken went back into the water. This time he heeded Helen's advice and consciously relaxed his tense body. He floated. He paddled to the left and then to the right. The longer he swam the more confident he became.

"Didn't I tell you swimming was easier than flying, eh?" said Helen.

Ken was elated. He could now not only fly but also swim.

"I can't believe I've conquered air and water

in addition to land! All thanks to you, Helen," said Ken fervently.

"Running, swimming, and flying maketh the complete bird. You are a quick learner, Ken. You made the effort, though, to be honest, it took some prodding. Now you must practice, practice, practice to perfect your swimming just as you did your flying."

"Do you know what goes best with today's victory?" Ken asked with a smile.

"No, what?"

"Listen to this," said Ken before breaking into Sinatra's 'High Hopes,' the anthem of positive thinking.

## 8 FATHER GOOSE, THE BIRD-MAN SAVIOR

After a flight and a swim with their small group, Helen and Ken were resting by the pond preening themselves and just enjoying the placid Sunday afternoon. Helen, as was her wont, stood on one leg but try as he might Ken could not imitate her. Just a few seconds on either leg was all he could manage before he thought he would topple over and quickly brought down the raised leg.

"Why is the farm so quiet?" asked Helen.

"Today is Sunday. You forgot? They have gone to church again. Tell me Helen, how do you spend your Sundays?"

"We leave town on Sundays. We fly out to nearby locales," replied Helen.

Ken grinned. "Don't tell me you go to multiple churches!"

"No, no. It's actually a church that forces us out. The one near our haunt in St. Catharines is as noisy as a rock band. Worship with ear-splitting music and strobe lights and all seems to me a strange concoction. Their racket drives us all nuts. We fly out for some peace and quiet to either Port Colborne, Niagara Falls, Port Dalhousie, or Gibson Lake."

"At least it is only once a week unlike the muezzin's calls five times a day, seven days a week," offered Ken.

"Nonetheless, it is good to cultivate quietness. The Creator listens to the silence of the heart."

"I doubt if the McGuires belong to a church like that," said Ken hazarding a guess.

"There are even bigger churches—mega churches, they call them—that can fill a hockey stadium. Difficult to tell where their sport ends and religion begins," smiled Helen.

"All churches are not the same, are they?" asked Ken.

"No, they are not. For one of them it seems no religion is the new religion. They don't believe there's a Creator. But they still go to church on Sundays and sing hymns. They have a minister. And there is even a sermon, But no Creator! All form and no substance," Helen said with a wry smile.

"Why do they do that?" Ken was puzzled.

"I have no idea! Sheer force of habit, I suppose. Or just plain make-believe."

"If they do not believe in the Creator, why waste their time continuing with the charade?" scoffed Ken.

"You know, they are mostly rich, well-to-do, educated intellectuals. Yet they believe with conviction that there is no Creator. They are fanatics of a liberal sort. Misguided but well-meaning do-gooders," Helen shook her head ruefully.

"How can they think that? Haven't they seen hurricanes and typhoons?" Ken wanted to know.

"And millions of tons of water and snow that fly through the air for thousands of miles without an engine? If only their blasted planes could do that, I would accept their belief," added Helen.

"They still think all this happened without a Creator? They must be as crazy as a loon ... no, I'll change that to coconut. As crazy as a coconut!"

"Do you know, one crazy atheist even implicated us?" Helen was indignant. "He said he does not believe in the Creator because he does not believe in Mother Goose. What stupidity!"

"We know better than that, don't we?"

"You know what is even more crazy? There are humans who don't believe in the Creator, but they have faith in the shadow of a groundhog."

"The one at Punxsutawney?" asked Ken.

Helen nodded.

"They even have a holiday for him every year! Can you believe that?" Helen laughed.

"You are pulling my leg now," said Ken in disbelief.

"No, I am not. But wait. There is more. There are people who worship cows, and elephants, and snakes. And even rats!"

"Now you are surely making this all up," said Ken skeptically.

"No, I'm not. Truth is stranger than fiction. There are even brilliant minds with a university education in their midst. Their deities are animals."

"Well … to each his own," Ken said with a shrug of his wings.

"I wish it were that simple. But do you know what some others do?"

"No. Next thing you'll tell me they worship rocks and stones."

"Precisely! Some of them actually do! They pay obeisance to sculptures and stone carvings," said Helen grimly. "But it gets worse. There are others who worship fellow humans as gods. How can anyone but the Creator be holy and inculpable? Then there are fanatics at the other end of the scale who are so intolerant that they believe slaughtering people of differing beliefs is a noble deed."

"What then is the true religion?" asked Ken.

"It is the faith of the fathers, devoid of all the modern claptrap of charlatans and pseudo mystics. It is the faith that reveres the Creator—not creation itself or the created. It is the faith of peace, love, and kindness—not of hate, violence, and bloodshed. It is the faith that does not desecrate the earth in its greed. It is the faith of humility and of deep tranquility and respect and tolerance for others."

"I wish I had a faith like that," Ken said wistfully.

"You already do— it's inside of you," was Helen's gentle response. "All you need to do is to bring it forth. Allow it to grow. Sorry to say, your elders have led you astray. We need to seek the original grace of the Creator. Instead, Man listens to rogues and charlatans who feed off the gullible by concocting fancy tales with their fertile imagination."

"I'm curious. Which of man's religions do you like the best?" asked Ken.

"Why, that's a no-brainer! The old believers, of course, with their adoration unchanged down the centuries. I go to pieces when I hear them chant of the wondrous works of the Creator."

*Upon the mountains, shall the waters stand,*
*Between the mountains, will the waters run.*

"Beautiful! But, come, let's go for another swim," suggested Ken.

+++

Helen decided it was time to tell Ken the story of the redemption of her tribe.

"I've been running down Man so much you might think they are our worst enemies," said Helen.

"They are not?" asked Ken quizzically.

"As a group, they are something awful but there are those who love us deeply. It was one of them that saved us," Helen said solemnly.

"Saved you? *Saved you?*" Ken was incredulous.

"Yes, saved us. He saved us from certain doom. From extinction. He was a godsend." Helen paused to collect her thoughts. "Yes, no doubt about it. He was clearly sent by the Creator to rescue us."

"Rescue you from what?" Ken was slightly exasperated.

"From ourselves. Our forebears slowly fell away from the faith of our fathers and from the traditions handed down to them. To begin with, they hunted us nearly to extinction. Then, they conspired to tame us. As I told you before, our wings were literally clipped. We could no longer fly. Memories of our annual southern pilgrimages began to fade from our institutional memory. Their unhealthy food almost killed us. We grew exceedingly obese. My forefathers became even more sluggish and lazy than the famed opium-eaters of the Orient. After physical indolence, it didn't take long for moral turpitude to set in. Chastity and fidelity were no longer considered virtues. Instead, promiscuity began to be considered the norm. Life had become a cabaret. There were worse sins beginning to sprout, like liaison of like with like, and like with unlike, if you get my drift, that I don't even want to mention. Like the Native Americans and the First Nations, we too had been deceived. We had lost our way in all senses of the term."

"What happened then? Ken could not endure the suspense.

"The cold first, and then the diseases of our own making, decimated us in captivity. Depression and deep despair were the order of the day. We were rudderless. And utterly lost. We were not just a gone case, we were gone geese, if you know what I mean. We even began to consider ourselves wiser than the Creator."

"What did Man do to save you?"

"Not Man in general. But just one man. Almost everyone considered him crazy. But he didn't care. He boldly stepped into the breach. He became one of us. He lived with us. He even flew with us!"

Ken laughed incredulously.

"*Flew* with you? I knew you were having me on. How can a man fly! What can be more farfetched and ridiculous than that? I can't imagine Patrick McGuire whirling around over the farm like a hot air balloon!"

Helen was nettled.

"This is no laughing matter. I'm serious. I'm telling you the unvarnished truth. All this really happened. It is the biggest event in our history since we were created."

Ken sobered up but was not able to completely

hide his skepticism.

"I'm not spinning a Mother Goose tale here," Helen continued. "This is a true story. It is the story of our redemption. If Father Goose—that is how we reverently called him, a name way better than bird-man, we thought—if Father Goose had not stepped in, I would not be here today. Not just me. None of my tribe. By all estimates we would have been on the brink of extinction by now, if not actually extinct. Or some genetically modified animal, a far cry from original state."

"But did he ... the Father Goose ... really fly?"

"That's the beauty of it. He actually did! But not on his own steam. He created this contraption called a microlight and gave it power. He would sit painfully cramped and hunched in this apparatus and fly around in the sky like a giant dragon fly. He took in my grandparents and their siblings when they were just-born goslings. He fed them and walked them around the grassy field and all the way to the clear waters of the small pond by his property. My ancestors adored him. They would follow him wherever he went. They even thought he was their mother! His love was imprinted in their hearts. And finally, he taught them to fly again."

"He did?"

"Yes, he did. He loved us more than anything else in this world. He would coo to the adopted goslings and talk to adult geese. Legend has it that he'd say, 'Talk to me goose!', as he egged each of them on to fly and reclaim their lost inheritance."

"He sounds like a very unique man to have loved your tribe so completely," pronounced Ken with a touch of jealousy.

"He was unique. There will never be another like him. His motives were completely altruistic. There was no money or fame in it. He showed us the way to redeem ourselves. He restored what my ancestors had thought had been lost forever. For, by then we had lost everything. Our self-esteem, our values, and our traditions, including the hallowed annual pilgrimage. We had neither the will nor the knowledge. So much so that we had forgotten even how to fly in a chevron! His greatest act was risking his life for us to show us the old way."

"To think a man would risk his life for a mere bird like us!" Ken exclaimed in awe.

"But he did! He encountered all the same dangers we face and more. On that first flight south with his wards, he flew ahead of them all the way from Ontario to Northern Virginia showing them the way. His microlight could have crashed to the earth anytime while our skein would still have been flying. There was nothing in it for him. What could we have given him in return? It was the purest act of selflessness. His own ilk thought he was crazy. He was derided and ridiculed. The Pharisaical government even tried to obstruct his efforts and labeled his good intentions as being dangerous for our welfare. Can you imagine the redeemer being dubbed a renegade!"

"But he won ultimately?" asked Ken.

"Of course, he did! I and my team down by the lake are living proof. We got our migration mojo going again. But a bigger miracle happened too. When we resumed our Creator-ordained custom of migration, the lost traditions and values were also magically gifted to us again, like fidelity and monogamy, honesty and diligence."

"The same qualities you said the Amish have."

"Yes, true. And the First Nations and the Native Americans too. There is a renaissance happening in their communities as well, away from drugs and alcohol."

"What an amazing, unbelievable story! But I believe you. Coming from anyone else I would have found it hard to keep a straight face through your narration."

"The worldly roll their eyes at the truth and think they are wise. They have more faith in Superman and Star Wars," Helen said dismissively.

"I wish someone would save our tribe too," sighed Ken.

"You don't need someone else. In essence, what Father Goose did works for all bird tribes. Talk to your elders and get them to rekindle the traditions they discarded or repressed for so long. They could connect cosmically with your tribe in East Asia to begin a collective awakening. Your lives will forever be transformed."

"I don't think that's going to be easy. I told you how my elders are," said Ken resignedly.

"I know. Enough talking. Let's go for a swim to Artemesia," suggested Helen.

Ken did not need a second invitation.

As they flew, they called down to Judy, Daniel, Nancy, and Bruce. Larry joined them again, flying on the right edge of the chevron, this time next to Helen. Not a word was said but Helen knew that Ken's presence was drawing Larry out to socialize again. The seven of them took the same route over Greenbelt Lake in Buddy Attick Park and Berwyn Heights to Lake Artemesia.

Ken frolicked in the water with the others. Being in the water was now a pleasurable experience. The fear of drowning was a distant memory.

After this flight, Larry approached Helen and Ken whenever they were close to pond. He never spoke a word but only acknowledged their presence by nodding. Days later, he began to fly with Ken and Helen on their sorties even if none of the others joined them. An unspoken bond was forming between the three.

While preening themselves by the pond shore, Ken said, "Flying is so powerful. I cannot imagine not flying."

"Yes, flying is indeed an amazing gift that we tend to take for granted. Did you know, we lose this power for more than ten percent of the year?" asked Helen.

"No, that can't be true!" exclaimed Ken.

"It is. It happens after our return journey right in the middle of summer—the best time of the year for flying and swimming. For forty days, we are grounded. We cannot fly."

"What stops you from flying? It is not as if you are caged or anything," Ken argued.

"No, it is nothing external. It is we ourselves.

We molt. We lose all our feathers. We become as powerless as a shorn Samson. We are at the mercy of our enemies. It is a period of abstinence and abject humility, while the rest of the world around us celebrates summer conspicuously."

"Why do you think this happens?" Ken asked.

"There can be different answers to that. The no-fly molting period is not an easy time. We are literally grounded. The inability to fly prevents us from foraging afar. We get by on much less food even while summer food is aplenty all around us. We are vulnerable and defenseless. I personally think molting serves to keep us humble and grateful. It is a time for introspection and renewal. When we can fly once again, it's like rebirth. It is sheer joy!"

"Do hunters go after you even when you are helpless?"

"Do you think anyone who carries a weapon of destruction will have even a drop of the milk of human kindness in them?"

"A sense of fairness perhaps?" ventured Ken.

"Bah! Their gunmen shoot even innocent schoolkids. They show no mercy. In some parts of this country nearly everyone has a gun. They even stock assault rifles at home. Those people are better armed than their police!"

"That is crazy! Makes no sense at all!" exclaimed Ken.

"Exactly! A weapon of violence can never be the instrument of peace. The proliferation of guns and violent deaths go hand in hand. But they just don't see it. They don't want to. I think it has become so bad, guns are needed now not to protect one's family as in olden days, but for protection *from* one's own family!"

"Terrible! But what about the Amish, the tribe you love?"

"They don't own Brownings, Gatlings, Kalashnikovs, or Uzis. The Amish use only old-fashioned rabbit rifles for hunting food. No machineguns or automatics for them."

"They are good in spite of their guns?" Ken did not sound convinced.

"The Amish way of life is the closest to ours. They are indubitably the best proponents of this planet. They do not intrude on others. They live close to the land and do not chase wealth and technology. Like us, their day starts with the sun and ends with it. Again, like us they pair for life. Their communities are well-knit and crime-free. They don't pollute. They are hard-working; there is no unemployment because everyone works; they take care of their elders; do not depend on government handouts—in a word they are self-reliant. All those are our values too."

"I think I will love the Amish too," Ken said.

They were silent for a while. Then Helen looked at Ken with a curious smile.

"What is funny?" asked Ken.

"I have just discovered irrefutable proof that guns and religion don't go together."

Ken looked skeptical. "Really? And you think the paid lackey congressmen of the NRA wouldn't have anticipated that already?"

"No, I'm pretty sure they haven't. This is original."

Ken said impatiently, "Go on, tell me. I can't wait to hear your theory."

"Here's my proof that guns and religion don't go together. The aim of these right-wing religious fanatics is to get saved and go to heaven, right? But they also love their guns and swear by their right to bear arms. Would you believe it, in some places they have more restrictions on fireworks than firearms?"

"Really?"

"Yes, indeed! Apparently being startled is worse than getting shot! They do not think straight. Here's my proof now," Helen said with an air of mystery.

"Come on, out with it!" urged Ken.

"Here it is. Remember you said the other day, there would be no killings in heaven? That set me thinking. If there are no killings, there would also not be any weapons—including guns—in heaven. Why would they need guns if there were to be no killings? Got that? I think even the NRA would not dispute that because they have no market in heaven! Ha, ha, ha. So, if there are no guns in heaven, and if the aim of the religious right is indeed to make a heaven on earth, where is the place for guns here?"

"Touché, Helen! Superb deduction!"

"And the other question that is nagging me is this: why would these gun-lovers want to go to heaven where there are no guns? There are only two commandments in heaven. There's no second amendment."

Ken laughed out loud.

"Nor a first, I might add," completed Helen.

Ken grinned from ear to ear. "Brilliant!" he cried flapping his wings.

But Helen had not finished. "I think it is fairly obvious that these gun lovers would be more at home in the other place where the smell of their gunpowder would in blend nicely with the odor fire and brimstone."

Ken doubled up in laughter, clapping his wings in merriment.

Helen turned serious. "Every time I think about the cruel hunter who shot Beth out of the skies and made a zombie out of Larry, my blood boils. Civilized, my foot!" she fumed in righteous anger.

## 9 THE CARNIVAL IS ENDING

Two days later tragedy struck.

It was mid-morning.

Ken's siblings and cousins, peers and compatriots, were nowhere to be seen. They had all wandered off in different directions, in search of food. Only Ken had stayed back. It was so quiet on the farm, he could hear the hum of the traffic on the Baltimore-Washington Parkway some distance away.

Ken knew Helen and her cohort would not be by the pond. She had told him the previous evening that Ruth, the team leader, had called a sortie this morning to the Conowingo Reservoir in Cecil County. The ticklish issue of Ken joining them on the trip had to be resolved. Ken had not flown with the larger group yet. While Ken and Helen debated what to do, the timing of the return clinched the issue for them. As Ruth had planned to return only after dusk, which would be past Ken's curfew hours at the farm, they both agreed that it would be safer for Ken to stay back than consider flying with the larger team.

"It will probably be too far for me anyway," Ken had himself admitted shrugging his shoulders, somewhat disappointed.

Though he knew that Helen and her group would not be there, Ken jumped the fence and went to the pond.

The team's nook was empty. Though there were other gaggles of Canada geese scattered around the pond, Ken felt a vague disquiet.

'It is not a place itself that one gets attached to. It is loving friends that make a place special— even a mundane place,' philosophized Ken as he headed back to the farm.

The absence of Helen weighed him down. He decided against going to the meadow in search of the others as he wanted to avoid the temptation of his former diet. Instead, he decided to potter around, whiling away the time till Helen's return, if perchance she returned early. Ken loitered aimlessly. Spring being still weeks away, there were no flowers to smell, no growing seedlings to observe.

His eating habits had been slowly transformed after meeting Helen. The previous craving for worms and insects had altered to a deep distaste for killing any living being. Ken had revamped and veganized his diet and was now, by choice, a confirmed herbivore.

The dead grass under the melted snow was not appetizing. Ken decided to wait for the evening meal of grain at the farm. He reverted to his favorite pastime of watching the streaking white lines in the azure sky. Ken tilted his head slightly to watch the comet-like vapor trails lengthen across the blue sky. Airplanes fascinated him.

That was when he intuitively sensed Ma's urgency without having seen or heard her. He became conscious of her anxiety. This was not the first time that he had had a presentiment like this. Mother and son shared a magic bond, communicating with each other wordlessly. It did not matter that they were several hundred feet from each other.

He left off watching airplanes to see Ma rushing helter-skelter towards him. Instead of her usual loud clucking that preceded a hurried arrival, it was a low, barely audible hissing. Her head down, wings flailing, Ma raced towards Ken in a tearing hurry like a charging quarterback.

"Ken, your life is in danger," gasped Ma, between pants, when she had reached him. "Their Super Bowl is this evening. They are going to kill two of our young ones."

"Are you sure, Ma? How do you know?" Ken still found it difficult to accept that Ryan's family to whom they gave all their eggs would kill and eat them.

"Don't argue. I was pecking for food in the open drain behind the kitchen. You know, where all the water from the sink flows out? Molly McGuire was washing the dishes after breakfast. I heard her tell her husband Patrick to kill two of us after church today."

Ken stood rooted to the spot.

"There is nothing I can do to protect you or your brothers," Ma continued. "They will spare your sisters for the eggs they will lay. I don't want you killed. I don't want any of my children killed. But you most of all. You are the son after my own heart. I have never had another child like you— and never will."

Ken had not seen his mother so emotional before.

"Go, save yourself. Stay out till sun set. Hide. Don't let a fistful of grain fool you. Their knives are out. Go now while the going is good. Get out!"

"I cannot leave you, Ma."

Ma wept her heart out. "It is my fate to see my children slaughtered. I cannot fight the beasts. They are giants. They are inhuman. Just go! Go save yourself." Ma wiped the tears away with her wings.

She threw her right wing over him in a hug. Ken hugged her back.

"Go now. Don't waste another minute," she urged him.

Ken did not need another prompt. "OK, Ma. I will do as you say. Stay safe, Ma," he whispered, his voice choking.

The next moment, he was airborne climbing in a low trajectory over the fence to the safety of the pond's edge on the other side. Ken crawled under the dry branches, to hide in the nooks and crannies where the partly unmelted snow lay.

Helen and her group did not get back before Ken's sunset curfew.

When he returned home as dusk was falling, he knew right away that the worst had happened. Sorrow hung heavy in the chicken shack like a pall of smoke on a winter's day. The usual commotion was conspicuous by its absence.

"They killed three of your brothers—not two. It was Dennis who cut their throats at the drain behind the kitchen. He even laughed as he decapitated them like an abominable terrorist. He is pure evil, that one. Stay far, far away from him."

"Where was Ryan when all this was happening?"

"There was a big fight between Ryan and Dennis before the killing started. Dennis announced that he wanted to kill the singer. That's you. And Ryan was vehemently against it. He ran around the farm looking for you ... to save you. When he did not find you, he left the house in a huff."

Ken scanned the shack for his brother and pal Joey. He was nowhere to be seen.

With a sinking feeling, Ken turned to Ma.

"Your brother Joey's gone, son. They tricked him with a handful of corn and slit his throat," she said bitterly. "They also executed your cousins Brad and Mark."

Ken was overcome with helpless anger. He decided he would not give up his life tamely when his time came. He would fight to the very end and not go gently without a struggle.

+++

Ken shared the sad tale with Helen the next day. Helen silently pondered over Ken's life in Greenbelt after she and the team returned to St. Catharines. She wished he would not have to go the way of all roosters.

Helen decided it was time to have a heart-to-heart talk with Ken.

"There's something I need to tell you. More like feedback or suggestion. Mixed with some unsolicited advice. Mind you, I'm not being judgmental," said Helen.

"With that kind of preface, I can guess what is coming. I bet it is some kind of racial slight or xenophobic insult."

"You still don't know me, do you? I'm not a racist. I've always had your best interests at heart. Always. Please don't get upset, Ken, at what I'm going to tell you. It is for your own good. Just don't take it personally. I will stick to facts and will not judge."

"It's not about my flying or swimming abilities, is it?"

"No, it's not. You are good at both. It has to do with the marriage customs of your tribe," said Helen.

"But we don't marry!" exclaimed Ken.

"Precisely! You just proved my point and saved me a lot of bother."

"But marriage is old-fashioned. It is outdated. Who needs marriage in this day and age?"

"For us Canada geese, marriage will never be out of fashion. It will remain forever. Our forebears handed it down to us and we will pass it on to the generations coming after us."

"But isn't it boring and staid?"

"Boring and staid? You aren't even married! What do you know of marriage?" queried Helen.

"You are single too. We're in the same boat," countered Ken.

"We consider our unions solemn and sacred. We partner for life. Till death. Forgive my saying this —again, I'm not being judgmental—but your tribe is as promiscuous as the philandering humans. Your males are a cheating, unfaithful bunch of fornicators who degrade the opposite sex merely as objects of lust."

"Don't put us in the same category as vile Man. We may have our frailties, but we don't have roosters consorting with roosters or hens with hens."

"Ha, ha! I'll grant you that! Neither do we, by the way. You know something else? They even teach this to their children in school. It is the craziest thing!"

"Really? You are kidding!" Ken was incredulous.

"No! They do. Instead of promoting chastity, they do the opposite. They encourage license and deviance."

"In children? Are you sure about this?" Ken found it hard to believe.

"It all has to do with their obsession about being politically correct that we talked about before. The desire to be seen as not being intolerant—even of deviancy. And do you know, they even lay the blame at our door?" Helen was indignant.

"They do?" Ken was surprised.

"Yes! They euphemistically refer to all this as the 'birds and the bees.' What an insult! If they learned from us, they would be much better off. Nobody can beat us when it comes to chastity and fidelity."

"Your tribe is more faithful and monogamous than Man. Come to think of it, one of you could run for the President of the United States," Ken said with a wink.

Helen looked at him blankly for a moment before it registered.

"Ah! On the grounds of chaste monogamy! Now wouldn't that be ironic, having a *Canada* goose as the *American* President!"

"The birthers will have a field day with your dual citizenship and your country of birth!" guffawed Ken.

+++

The days continued getting longer and the nights a tad shorter than the preceding. There was a still a nip in the air, but the cold had already fled up north. Spring was just around the corner.

Helen hummed *'Way Up North'* in unconcealed happiness.

"Spring is in the air!" she gushed in anticipation.

Ken, though, was morose.

"What's the matter with you? You prefer the icicles of Siberia, eh?" Helen was cross.

"Helen, you don't get it, do you? You can be so heartless at times. You are going to go back to Canada in a few weeks," Ken blurted out.

"Yes, but I'll be back next fall! It's going to be just six months or even less," she said. "In the meantime, you can fly around and enjoy the warm summer. You will be the lone flying chicken for miles around. You'll be famous!" she added feigning enthusiasm.

"Easy for you to say," Ken retorted. "I could end up on the table long before that. Any day they could chop my neck off and stick me in the oven," Ken grumbled in sullen anger. "A fat good the flying will do then. I'll be frying—not flying!"

Helen was dumbstruck.

After a long pause, she said solemnly, "It's not as if our three-day journey is going to be a cakewalk. Some of us, as it happened with Beth, may not make it."

It was Ken's turn to speak his mind.

"Helen, do you even realize how much you mean to me? There is danger ahead for both of us. But if you stay, at least we will be together when the end comes. Don't go!" he pleaded plaintively.

"Ken, but that's impossible! I cannot stay even if I want to! I must go with my tribe to the land of our birth. It is a sacred and inviolable tradition."

Ken could only stare back, tears welling in his eyes.

Helen tried to console him. "Ken, you know how

much I hate to leave you. I love you. If there was any way ..."

She paused suddenly. Her face lit up with the excitement of a thousand idea bulbs popping in her head.

"I have a proposition to make," she said with studied nonchalance, a trace of conspiratorial glint in her eyes.

"Why don't you come with me? With us, I mean. To Canada." Helen asked with a faint smile on her lips.

Ken was dumbfounded.

Helen's smile turned broader as she crooned, "Come fly with me to Canada ... let's fly away ..."

"Are you out of your mind?" Ken blurted out when he had found his voice.

"It is not out of the realms of possibility. Why must we confine our thinking to pre-set boundaries? Remember what we talked about once? Let's fly in the face of presumption and achieve victory! Let's put it to the test!" she said defiantly.

"Do you think this is some kind of a joke? How can I fly that far?"

"Am I suggesting that you change into an

elephant or a giraffe or a whale or a snake or a barnacle? They are of different genres entirely. You and I are birds. You can fly now and swim. All I'm suggesting is that you exercise the freedom of choice you have now. Why be a slave to cruel Man who cares only about his stomach? If you don't watch out, you would soon be a buffalo chicken."

"A *buffalo*?" Ken was incredulous.

"More like buffalo wings, actually," said Helen with a giggle. "They are the staple of Super Bowls. The name comes from Buffalo, New York. Coincidentally, that's the first US city we overfly coming down here in the fall from Canada. They even celebrate a buffalo wing week there."

"Are you trying to scare me?" Ken was annoyed.

"Let me lay all the cards on the table. If you stay back here, you will certainly die an early death like your brothers. The Aerial Flyway to Canada is risky, I agree, as it was for those on the Underground Railroad. But at least it has the possibility of freedom. The way I see it, you have nothing to lose and everything to gain. Why don't you give it a shot? I will help you all I can. At least you would have tried. As I always say, the bigger failure is never trying. You would not only have not achieved but would also have to live, however briefly, with the guilt of lacking the gumption to take a no-brainer gamble."

She paused before adding, "Fear of failure is the only fence between heaven and hell, between bondage and freedom."

"But I cannot fly a thousand miles," lamented Ken.

"O, yes, you can! And it's actually only about five hundred as the goose flies. Ha, ha. Remember we don't fly the whole distance in one day. We stretch it over three days, or even more depending on the weather and flying conditions. By now you can fly as well as the best of us. You have been relentless in your training. Let me ask you something. Did you train so hard in the secret hope of flying with us to Canada?"

"No! That did not even cross my mind! I just wanted to be the best flying chicken there was in the world. That is what Ma taught me. To try to be the best at everything I did."

"That's a good attitude to have," commended Helen. "My guess is all you need to do is to step your stamina up another notch. We can train together for that. But, sorry I completely overlooked something. Aren't we putting the cart before the horse here, eh? I'll have to talk to

Ruth first."

Ken was not hopeful.

"I don't think Ruth will agree to take me on. This whole idea is so preposterous she will think you are crazy," Ken said despondently.

"Ken, we have got to will things that we want to happen. If we have the teeniest bit of doubt in our minds, the wish will not come to pass. What have we got to lose here, eh? Nothing!"

"You know what gives me hope? If Ruth agreed and I did make it, I would get to see the Niagara Falls."

"Not just see it, you can fly circles over the Falls to your heart's content."

+++

Ken could not get a private moment with Ma that night in the shack. But the next morning as Ma waited alone indoors to lay the day's egg, Ken sidled up to share his plans.

"I'm planning to leave, Ma," he said choking on the words.

"Have they decided on the departure date already?" she asked arching her eyebrow.

Ken was again astonished by Ma's intuition.

"How did you know I was leaving with them?

Come to think of it, why must I be surprised?"

She only smiled.

"Anyway, nothing is certain yet. Their leaders have to approve. Ma, you will let me go, won't you?" Ken pleaded.

"Son, I have always encouraged you to grow and live life your way. I will not block your path now. What future do you have here anyway? A few more weeks and you will be dinner, unless Ryan has his way, and he can't hold out forever."

Ken remembered his murdered brother Joey.

"Thank you, Ma. You are the best mother anyone could have. If the Canada geese choose to admit me to their club, I will go with them. If they turn me down, I will still leave, and live on the lam. I would rather take my chances than meekly surrender to certain death."

+++

"How do you know your way back to St. Catharines?" wondered Ken.

"Our sense of direction is better than a GPS. We use the stars and the moon—not satellites. The veterans pass on their knowledge to the first timers. Once you have made a trip, the route is imprinted on our minds forever."

"That's amazing! Do you use the North Pole or the North Star as a reference?" asked Ken.

"Funny you should ask that. We believe that everyone, whether on land, in the water, or in the air, needs to find his or her True North," Helen said gravely.

"What if they cannot find it?" Ken was unsure what Helen was referring to.

"All who search, will find. That's an absolute certainty," Helen said with certainty.

"How can you be so sure?" Ken was not convinced.

"Because the True North is of the Creator," Helen pronounced solemnly. "It's the yellow brick road of life."

"Whoa! That's deep! And what happens when they do find it?" Ken was wide awake.

"When individuals find their True North, they will begin to lead successful lives. Successful not by worldly standards but in terms of fulfillment and satisfaction, and enriching—not oneself—but others and the world that we live in."

"Where do I go to search for the True North?"

"Here's the beauty of it. You can be in Paris or

Kabul. In Ouagadougou or Wagga Wagga. The place where you are matters little because there is only one True North. You can find it anywhere you are."

"I want to find mine," Ken said eagerly.

"You will, Ken. And that sooner than you think. You are halfway there already."

"Helen, this cannot wait."

"I've been thinking also. I think I now have a better idea of who or what I am. Neither an expat, nor an asylum-seeking refugee. Not an interloper or a fugitive. Neither a malefactor nor a masquerader. I already knew I wasn't a dunce or a thaumaturge. Now I know, I'm not a guru or a sensai, either."

"What are you then, Helen?" Ken enquired.

"I'm actually a subaltern cosmopolitan, outside as I am of the cultural hegemony of any country. To be more precise, I'm an apatetic subaltern cosmopolitan. Apatetic—not apathetic, mind you—because, as a dedicated code-switcher, I blend with the mores of the place where I am without deviating from my own True North."

Ken's eyes bulged. "It will take me a long time to get my head around that!" As he turned away, he added, "But whether our crazy plan works out or not, you will always be just Helen to me. And that is saying a lot."

## 10 Nothing Left To Lose

When Helen sought a private conversation, Ruth's response was firm.

"However confidential the subject is, we need to include Hoover. He is as much the leader of this team as I am. If it's urgent, I'll see if we can meet tonight."

Before turning in for the night, the three met by the pond shore.

"I will not beat about the bush," started Helen. "This has to do with Ken."

"Don't tell me you have decided to stay back?" Ruth did not hide her dismay.

"No, I wouldn't dream of doing that. I have no intention of going against our customs and traditions. But at the same time, I do not want to leave Ken to his fate. He will be killed for sure."

"Helen, I understand your concern but there is little we can do. We cannot be the police force of the world."

"No, I did not mean that, Ruth." Helen paused to take a deep breath. "I would like your permission for Ken to accompany us to St. Catharines," Helen stated plainly.

"What!" gasped Ruth, taken aback. "That's impossible! He is not a goose. He can't fly like us."

Hoover did not speak but only smiled wisely. Helen continued.

"Agreed, Ken is not a goose, but he is a bird like us. And he has learned to fly. He can now fly like the best of us. He can swim too. He has worked really, really hard to redeem himself. Please, Ruth, consider!" pleaded Helen.

Ruth and Hoover looked at each other before Ruth spoke again.

"This is unheard of. Canada geese enlisting a Rhode Island Red chicken? This is very, very unusual. Never been done before. You know the risks. Ken may not come out of this trip alive. But still, Hoover and I will consider this with an open mind. I'm not saying yes or no at this stage. What are your thoughts, Hoover?"

Hoover spoke with calm deliberateness.

"That Ken is a chicken does not matter to me. I do not have any objections per se on that count. Of his being a different kind of bird. But he must have the capacity to reach the finish line. What we need to be certain is that by taking Ken on, we are not putting his life in danger. Nor ours. We cannot afford to take too many risks outside of reasonable accommodation."

"What are you suggesting, Hoover?" asked Ruth.

"Whichever way we decide, our decision must be objective. Must be rational. I think we need to assess Ken's skills and ability and base our decision solely on that," Ken replied.

"That's sounds reasonable. Can you take care of the assessment, Hoover?" Ruth suggested.

"Hmm ..." Hoover cocked his head in thought. "I've known Ken since he first came visiting a week after our arrival. In recent days, I've watched him fly with our juniors. He can fly better than the youngsters now. I am certain he'll easily pass the mental and psychological hurdles. Otherwise he wouldn't have come this far. What I need to be sure of is his stamina and physical endurance. He was not born one of us and his physique is different. The only test I would put him to is a test of stamina and endurance."

Helen was overjoyed. "Thank you! Thank you!" she gushed. "I'm sure he will pass the test."

"Let me be the judge of that," said Hoover good-naturedly. "That said, I will be happy if he comes through. I like triers. We'll give him a fair chance."

Helen could not wait to tell Ken.

+++

When they met the next morning, Helen related the previous evening's meeting to Ken.

"Ruth and Hoover are willing to take you with us. But you need to take a test."

Ken recoiled at the idea. "What kind of test? They'll fail me I'm sure."

"It's a test of flying. Should be a piece of cake for you!" Helen tried to sound upbeat.

"I don't like this. I don't do well in tests," Ken said scowling.

"Don't be so diffident and pessimistic! Don't underestimate yourself. You have what it takes. Worst case scenario, what have you got to lose? Give it a try. If you pass—and I have no doubt you will—a whole new world will open for you. You won't have to wait a half year to see me. Nor I you. We will make the journey together. And you'll get to see the Niagara Falls. Just think!"

Ken fell for Helen's pitch hook, line, and sinker.

"Time is of the essence. Let me talk to Hoover," she said when he consented. Helen flew back while Ken waited under the oak tree.

Hoover was most accommodating.

"We can do it any day Ken is ready. But I'd rather do it sooner rather than later."

Helen returned to Ken's side with the good news.

+++

When Ken arrived right after breakfast the next morning, there was Hoover and Helen along with a small group comprised of the usual suspects— Judy and Daniel, Nancy and Bruce, and Larry.

Hoover jumped right into it.

"Helen, you lead us. We will fly first to Annapolis and then to the Chesapeake Bay."

Larry, Ken, and Hoover formed the left wing of the chevron with Ken in the middle. The other four made up the right wing. Hoover took the vantage position slightly behind and to the left of Ken, so he could keep an eye on how he was doing.

Annapolis was easy, but they flew on, not

touching ground. On reaching the Bay, they flew up to Ocean City first and then down to Virginia Beach nonstop. When they finally landed on Kent Island, they had been flying without a break for nearly four hours. Hoover noted that they were all a tired lot, but Ken still looked good for a some more flying.

For the return to Greenbelt, Hoover was pleased to see Larry voluntarily switch places with Helen. Larry was slowly coming out of his shell.

Ruth was waiting for them when they reached home base. They coasted down to gently alight in front of her. She read the result right away on Hoover's face.

Ken waited in suspense for the verdict when Hoover turned to him.

"Ken, you passed with flying colors!" Hoover did not hold back on his praise. "You did very well indeed."

Then, turning to Ruth, he said, "Over to you," with a nod signifying approval.

Ruth wasted no time or words.

"Congratulations, Ken! You are on! You are invited to join us on our journey back to Canada as an honorary member of our team."

The four juniors Nancy, Bruce, Judy, and

Daniel collected around him to compliment him. Larry stayed where he was but waved.

Ken was elated. 'Yes! He had qualified to fly with the elite Canada geese!'

He mumbled a hasty 'Thank you!' and took leave of them, literally jumping over the fence in a fancy straight drop into the backyard of the farm.

He whizzed like a rocket to the pasture on the far side of the farm house where Ma was foraging with the others. He did not mind the lack of privacy.

"Ma, I passed the test!"

"I had no doubt you would," Ma said matter-of-factly but with obvious pride.

Ken began to say something more, but Ma intervened.

"Let's talk this over later in the evening at home."

Ken was a little disappointed but flew back to Helen's side by the pond. They needed some time alone to celebrate this extraordinary milestone. They flew, just the two of them, to Lake Artemesia. In the cool waters of the lake, the aches and pains of the arduous test flight dissipated. As he lifted his head out of the water after a dunk, Ken marveled at how much he now loved the waters that he once feared. He practiced again the one maneuver he still had a bit of a problem with—tipping over head first to hold his head under water.

"You are getting there but you probably need a little bit more practice on that move," Helen said.

The long talk with Ma that he was mentally preparing for did not happen that night. He wondered if Ma was deliberately avoiding any prospect of a private discussion.

+++

On the directions of Ruth and Hoover, there followed long training flights every other day. After one such sortie, Larry sidled over quietly and opened up to Ken.

"You are doing very well, Ken!" Larry said out of the blue.

"Why, thank you, Larry!" stammered Ken.

Larry had moved way as quietly as he had come.

Helen who was nearby made an offhand remark that startled Ken.

"There is a destiny that shapes our ends," she

said casually.

"Destiny? Are you a fatalist, Helen?" asked Ken.

"Do you think on my own it would even cross my mind to fly a thousand miles to come here? Or, of all places, my team would choose Greenbelt, Maryland, instead of, say, Asheville, North Carolina?"

"You are confusing me. Then what is destiny?"

"I strongly believe there is a universal scheme of things, a divine plan so to speak, in which each one of us has a role to play."

"Then we are just actors playing out a script?"

"Wait. I did not finish. There is the universal scheme or divine plan. And then there's the individual free will to opt in or opt out. If we strive to do good to others and to the world that is given to us, life, nature, and seemingly random occurrences will all collude together in our favor to make our life truly a life well-lived."

"You really believe that?" asked Ken.

"Of course, I do. The opposite is true as well. If we live isolated, selfish, egotistic lives exploiting nature and neighbors to satisfy our own egocentric desires, then misery, ennui, and depression are the results."

"You are saying, that there is a purpose to our meeting?" Ken pushed on.

"Of course, there is!" said Helen vehemently with conviction. Then she added with a smile, "If nothing else, at least a beautiful friendship."

Ken's adoration did not need words.

That evening Ken caught Ma alone in a corner of the shack.

Saying goodbye to Ma turned out to be far more difficult for Ken than for Ma.

"Ma, I'll soon be ..." he began but his voice cracked with emotion.

"Ken, you are only leaving—not dying."

"To be away from you is a fate worse than death," Ken said dejectedly.

"Now, stop being sentimental. You think I am happy with goodbyes? If we are lucky, yours will be the first and likely only goodbye. I never get a chance to say a word of farewell to any of my children before they are dragged off to the knife."

"Sorry, Ma."

"We are made of sterner stuff than our murderers. You are leaving us. That is the sad part. But I'm overjoyed that you will be escaping your fate. You will no longer be a victim of your circumstances. I will always be proud of you and your achievements. By the way, when are you leaving?"

"No dates have been set yet. But I think it will be soon."

"Come sit by me," Ma said.

They sat side by side without a word. To Ken it felt like old times.

+++

The next day's training run took them around Baltimore-Washington airport to Linthicum, Glenburnie and Whitby's Landing. After rest and refreshments, they flew to the Patapsco River and finally to the Inner Harbor in Baltimore. From the grassy lawns near Fort McHenry they watched the milling crowds on the waterfront promenade and the ships and boats on the water.

"I now see how big ships can be," admitted Ken sheepishly.

"You will like the Great Lakes even better," replied Helen.

By the time they were airborne again for home, the city lights had come on. The bright lights disoriented Ken. He panicked. To make matters worse, the turbulent jet wash of an airplane that had just taken off from Baltimore Washington International airport slammed into them. A blast of hot gases and acrid fumes enveloped them. Helen, flying next to him, came to his rescue.

"Steady on! The turbulence will last only a minute or two. And those blinding lights will be behind us in a little while," she yelled over the roar of engines and the traffic below.

When they reached the pond, Ruth and Hoover had news for them. Hoover nodded for Ruth to make the announcement.

"We are leaving in three days. The weather has warmed up enough. There is a hurricane forecast for this area for the coming weekend. We can beat it if we leave on Tuesday."

"The prediction is for a hot summer this year," interjected Hoover. "St. Catharines should be warm enough already."

"Yes, that's right, Hoover," continued Ruth. "We will have a team meeting tomorrow. To accommodate Ken who has an early curfew—he is already late today—the meeting will be in the morning instead of late afternoon."

Ken flew home with mixed emotions, the excitement of new frontiers and the sadness of leaving family and home.

+++

The next morning Hoover convened the meeting.

"Order! Order! Order! Let us, as we always do, observe a moment of quiet gratitude before we begin. We've been here for half a year."

After the silent pause, Ruth began.

"Thank you, Hoover. I begin with a special announcement. Hoover and I decided that we will have four, instead of the usual three, staging posts on our return journey to St. Catharines. As you all know by now, Ken has been invited to join our team and will be flying with us. He has trained earnestly and believe he is fully prepared for the long journey. But we do not want to put too much of a strain on him. We will space the return journey out a bit."

There was an unexpected interruption from Larry that surprised everyone.

"Ruth and Hoover and everybody else. I did not say anything before, but I just want to say how glad I am that we're taking Ken along. I have known what it is to be lonely and alone. I move that we do all we can to make Ken feel at home with us."

This was the first time in a year that Larry had publicly voiced his opinion on anything.

"Thank you, Larry, for speaking up. We will certainly do all we can for Ken." Ruth looked at Ken. "Welcome to our team, Ken! From now on you are one of us. It does not matter at all that you are a handsome Rhode Island Red rooster. We won't hold that against you." Everyone laughed. "What is important is your desire to join us. You are an equal member of our team now. Let's give Ken a round of applause."

When the honks and the wing flapping had died down, Ruth continued.

"But here's the second surprise and it is just for you, Larry. The extra stop we will be making will be on the shores of the Finger Lakes in New York State. Hoover and I decided we would hold a brief memorial there for Beth who was dear to all of us, and most of all to you."

Larry, overcome by emotion, could only mumble an incoherent thanks.

"Tomorrow, Sasha, our seven-time veteran, and Fritz, who has been on four trips, will do a recon flight just to confirm that the coast is clear. It will be rest and preparation from now on before we depart Greenbelt in the evening the day after tomorrow."

When they were alone, Ken asked Helen.

"Will we be overflying my namesake state?"

"Unfortunately, not. The state of Rhode Island is a little further to the right than our route. We will be flying over Pennsylvania State for the most part with a final lap over the State of New York to the edge of Lake Erie. From there it is just half a hop home to the province of Ontario."

+++

On the appointed day, the sun had just dipped below the still leafless tree tops silhouetted against the orange horizon fading upwards into the deepening steel gray canopy when Ken hugged Ma goodbye.

Their hearts were as heavy as the odds against their seeing each other again.

"I'll be back next fall with the Canada geese," Ken assured Ma.

Ma fought back the doubts that enveloped her. She wanted to believe Ken's words, that they would meet again.

"I know you will, Ken. You are as good a flier as the rest of them. Just don't take any unnecessary risks. Stick close to Helen. I will always love you. You have made me proud."

"Ma, I love you too. I always will."

With that he quietly slipped out of the shack pausing to take one last look at the farm house. The kitchen window was lit. Ken guessed the family must be at their supper. He fondly gazed at the grassy knoll in the middle of the meadow and the trees beyond. So many memories. He knew Ryan would be heart-broken in the morning when he found him gone.

"Goodbye, Ryan! You are a good man! I'm going to miss you. Sorry to be leaving without a goodbye but this chicken has got to do what he has got to do," whispered Ken softly.

He half-wanted to sing a sad song of farewell, but it was too late in the evening to be singing.

Ken flapped his wings gently in a wave of goodbye.

Then with a powerful swish he was airborne, climbing steeply to clear the chain-link fence to glide like a pro to the edge of the pond where Helen awaited him.

+++

"Helen, I can't believe this is actually happening. I hope I won't bring disgrace upon the team."

"You and I, we know you can do this, right?" encouraged Helen.

"Yes, of course," intoned Ken hesitantly but

quickly banished the misgivings that had again resurfaced. "Yes, I can! I want to see the Falls!"

Then he added jokingly, "I will get to cross that off my bucket-list very soon!"

"Yeah! That's the spirit! Canada here we come!" Helen bubbled with infectious enthusiasm.

"Yay! Canada!" echoed Ken with gusto.

He remembered Ryan then.

"I'm going to miss Ryan. Hope he doesn't worry that I've been killed by a coyote or a fox."

"Have no fear of that. He has been watching you fly with us. When he finds that we have gone too, he will put two and two together. He will know you've flown the coop—and the country!"

Soon Ruth and Hoover signaled the group to assemble.

"As is our custom, let's all sit down quietly for a few moments before this long journey to thank the Creator of all for the blessings we've enjoyed here in Greenbelt. Let's rest in gratitude and in hope," pronounced Ruth softly.

After the silent meditation, she continued.

"It's going to be a long flight, as we all, including Ken, already know. None of us can fly solo that far. We all need each other. That's why we fly the chevron. We will switch places to share the strain of leading. Remember what I said on the way down: we are each of us the other's wingman. Or for that matter, wingwoman. Hoover?"

"I have nothing much to add. Let's fly safe—as a team! If anyone needs a last bite or drink—or a bathroom break—this is the time. Let's assemble again in fifteen minutes."

The group scattered quickly. Ken walked with Helen to the edge of the pond for a last drink.

"The water is cold, but it tastes so good," marveled Ken as he raised his head to let the water flow down into his belly.

When they reassembled, limbering up for the voyage, a cool wind blew gently from the north. The darkened sky was lightening again with the full moon rising. They took up positions close to each other.

Hoover fired up the group up with some spirited cheering.

"Let's go! Let's head on home! Canada! O, Canada! Here we come!"

"Yay! Yay!" echoed the group.

"All ready?" yelled Hoover.

They took their assigned positions. Ken was the last on the left side, right next to Helen. To her right was Larry. Helen gave Ken a reassuring smile.

"One, two, here we go!" Hoover boomed.

They were off. A few steps running, and then they were airborne, rising steadily against the head wind. Over Buddy Attick Park and Greenbelt Lake, then over Lake Artemesia, they flew in a chevron climbing higher and higher like a just-released boomerang. Soon they were higher than the highest Ken had ever been. The temperature and the force of gravity both declined in unison as they climbed still higher.

The cool wind in his face was the taste of freedom that he had longed for. Ken felt alive and free as the supreme joy of actualization possessed him.

He began to sing. Helen turned to look at him, as he flew slightly behind her, to her left.

"Are you *singing*?" Helen was incredulous.

Ken winked and raised his voice as he joyfully sang, *'Ain't No Mountain High Enough'* ...

## EPILOGUE

So it was that Ken, by birth and upbringing a Rhode Island Red rooster, by daring to dream the improbable, surpassed the boundaries he was given, fulfilled his latent potential, reclaimed his lost heritage, and transformed himself into—not a gander of Helen's ilk, the Canada geese—but a redeemed fowl, to take his rightful place amongst the league of champions who traverse the skies.

# The Migrant and the Maverick

**Father goose, the Bird-Man Savior**

William Lishman, nonconformist, artist, inventor, and nature lover, of Ontario, Canada, believed that for migratory birds raised in captivity to survive, they needed to be trained to migrate, a skill they had lost. He pioneered aircraft-led migration using microlights to lead a gaggle of Canada geese from Ontario to Virginia in 1993.

The feat was documented in the award-winning film, *C'mon Geese*.

The 1996 commercial film *Fly Away Home* starring Jeff Daniels and Anna Paquin is based on this true story of Bill Lishman and his microlight-led migration of home-raised Canada geese.

**Postscript**

Sadly, Bill passed away in December 2017, a few months after he had given his permission for mentioning his story in this book.

The author welcomes comments at:

aa-books@outlook.com


For more information about the author's books:

www.abiealexander.com

www.ingramcontent.com/pod-product-compliance
Lightning Source LLC
Chambersburg PA
CBHW061229170626
46809CB00007B/2581